THE ALL-NEW
MALLORY PIKE

Other books by
Ann M. Martin

P.S. Longer Letter Later
(written with Paula Danziger)
Leo the Magnificat
Rachel Parker, Kindergarten Show-off
Eleven Kids, One Summer
Ma and Pa Dracula
Yours Turly, Shirley
Ten Kids, No Pets
Slam Book
Just a Summer Romance
Missing Since Monday
With You and Without You
Me and Katie (the Pest)
Stage Fright
Inside Out
Bummer Summer

THE KIDS IN MS. COLMAN'S CLASS series
BABY-SITTERS LITTLE SISTER series
THE BABY-SITTERS CLUB mysteries
THE BABY-SITTERS CLUB series
CALIFORNIA DIARIES series

THE ALL-NEW
MALLORY PIKE

Ann M. Martin

AN
APPLE
PAPERBACK

SCHOLASTIC INC.
New York Toronto London Auckland Sydney
Mexico City New Delhi Hong Kong

Cover art by Hodges Soileau

No part of this publication may be reproduced in whole or in part, or stored in a retrieval system, or transmitted in any form or by any means, electronic, mechanical, photocopying, recording, or otherwise, without written permission of the publisher. For information regarding permission, write to Scholastic Inc., Attention: Permissions Department, 555 Broadway, New York, NY 10012.

ISBN 0-590-50349-9

12 11 10 9 8 7 6 5 4 3 2 1   9/9 0 1 2 3 4/0

Printed in the U.S.A.   40
First Scholastic printing, January 1999

*The author gratefully acknowledges
Ellen Miles
for her help in
preparing this manuscript.*

CHAPTER 1

January 2. The holidays are over. Now I can turn my mind to the next event in my life. I, Mallory Pike, am about to embark on the biggest journey I've taken so far. Not the longest — this trip will only take me as far as Massachusetts — but definitely the biggest. I am about to start a whole new life.

I am going away to boarding school.

I stared down at the page in my journal, trying to grasp the reality of the words.

In two days, instead of going back to Stoneybrook Middle School with my friends, I'd be heading to Riverbend Hall, a private, all-girls boarding school, to finish out my sixth-grade year. And hopefully to stay through high school. I was excited, and terrified, and happy, and sad — a big tangle of emotions.

See, I've lived all eleven years of my life in Stoneybrook, Connecticut. I love the nine other members of my family (I have seven siblings!), and I have the best friends anyone could imagine. Including Jessi Ramsey, my very best friend. (She and I are junior members of the Baby-sitters Club, or BSC. More about that later.)

It wasn't going to be easy to leave my home and family and friends, but I'd thought over my decision for a long time, and I was as sure as I possibly could be that I was doing the right thing.

It was Thursday night, and quiet in the Pike house for a change. My parents had taken my brothers and sisters to the movies in order to give me some time on my own. I'd been packing all day and I was worn-out. It wasn't easy to decide what to take with me, and it definitely wasn't easy to fit everything into one big trunk and a small suitcase.

Finally, I decided I'd done enough for one

day. I plopped down on my bed and pulled out my journal from under my mattress.

Writing in my journal is essential to me. It's something I do nearly every day, and it's almost as if the day isn't complete until I've recorded my thoughts and feelings about what's happened. I've always loved to write. In fact, I plan to be a writer when I grow up — a writer and illustrator of children's books, to be exact. (I love to draw too.)

It won't be long now. Two more nights in my own bed. By Saturday night I'll be sleeping in a new bed, at Riverbend Hall. I can't even begin to imagine what my life there will be like. And what about life here, without me? It won't grind to halt, I know that. But will I be missed? Will my absence be noticed? I wonder...

As I sat on the floor, leaning against my bed with the journal in my lap, I stopped writing and began to daydream. I was imagining life in Stoneybrook without Mallory Pike. It was as if I were floating invisibly through a day sometime in the future, watching my family and friends go on with their lives while I was at Riverbend.

"Mom, tell Nicky to stop chewing with his mouth open! I'm going to barf if he doesn't quit."

"Go, Nicky! Show her more!"

Ah, yes. A family dinner, Pike-style. That was the first thing I imagined. And so far, nothing much had changed. Nicky, who's eight, was doing his best to gross everyone out. Margo, the one who said she'd barf, is seven. She's always had a weak stomach. And who was encouraging Nicky? Adam, of course. He's one of the triplets, my ten-year-old brothers. Jordan and Byron are the other two. In my daydream, Byron was playing with a long strand of spaghetti, sucking it in and squirting it back out, sucking it in again and squirting it out. Jordan was counting as he watched. "Eight, nine, ten! You're going for a world record, man!" he said, pounding Byron on the back.

"Ew," said Claire, my youngest sibling. She's five. "Boys are so gross. Spaghetti is for eating, you silly-billy-goo-goo Byron!" She sucked in her own strand of spaghetti so fast that tomato sauce splashed on her face.

"What rhymes with spaghetti?" my sister Vanessa asked as she dreamily twirled a few strands around her fork. "Petty? Letty?" she tried. "That's a tough one." Vanessa, who's nine, wants to be a poet. She loves to think up rhymes.

My mom and dad were basically ignoring the whole scene. Oh, they threw in an occasional "Use your napkin, Claire," or "Chew with your mouth closed, Nicky," but mostly they tried to act as if this were a civilized dinner with civilized people, just as they've always done.

It's a losing battle.

But I could have helped. I would have wiped Claire's face and helped to cut up her spaghetti so she wouldn't have made such a mess of herself. I would have offered several rhymes to Vanessa ("Betty" came to mind), distracted Margo so Nicky would have no reason to show off and Adam would have no reason to egg him on. And I would have informed Byron that he was nowhere near creating a world's record. (The spaghetti-sucking record was set years ago by my friend Kristy's brother Sam, who did it twenty-seven times.)

My family. There they were, all of them around the table. Nine Pikes, all with brown hair and blue eyes. I'm the only one who doesn't quite match, since my hair is reddish-brown and much curlier than anyone else's. Vanessa and Nicky wear glasses, like I do (I'm dying for contacts, but my parents say I have to wait until I'm fifteen), but nobody else wears braces (yuck).

There wasn't even an empty chair for me; instead they'd put mine away and spread out so everyone had a little more space. I couldn't blame them. In a family as big as ours, we're always looking for more space.

Suddenly, in my daydream, Byron looked up at my dad. "I wonder what Mal's doing right now," he said thoughtfully.

"Having a nice, quiet dinner, probably," my dad answered jokingly.

"I miss Mal," said Claire. "When will she be back?"

"Not for awhile," said my mom, patting Claire's hand. "And I miss her too. We all do." She looked sad.

"Right," said Nicky. "So, can I have her dessert tonight?"

I burst out laughing. My daydream had seemed so real. I knew that's just how it would be. My family would miss me, but they'd go on as they always had.

That's my family! Same as ever. But what about school?

School. That was another matter. I wasn't sure I even wanted to daydream about school. I hadn't been happy there recently. In fact, imagining life at SMS was more like a day-*nightmare*. Still, I let myself drift off, picturing myself floating through the school, invisibly observing the place I was leaving behind.

The halls were filled with kids. Homeroom

was over, and everyone was on their way to first period. People were jostling one another as they rushed to class. Lockers slammed and kids shouted to each other.

"Hey, where's Spaz Girl?" I heard a boy call. "I haven't seen her in awhile."

"Spaz Girl?" someone answered. "She's probably spazzing around somewhere."

A girl laughed uproariously at his remark.

Ugh. They're talking about me.

You see, I am Spaz Girl.

I *was* Spaz Girl.

That was the nickname some eighth-graders gave me after a disastrous episode in which I tried my hand at student teaching. It was a special program at SMS, and if I'd been smart I would have avoided it. Instead, I wanted to be part of it, but some stupid things happened, and a couple of jerks started to call me Spaz Girl. Soon the word spread, and the nickname stuck. Before long, kids were scrawling it on my locker and yelling it at me in the halls. I hated it, hated it, hated it.

There were other problems too. In my daydream, I pictured one of my teachers talking about me.

"She stopped trying," said Mr. Zizmore, my math teacher. "She used to get such good grades, but now . . ."

I lost confidence and stopped being able to

focus on my schoolwork. Spaz Girl wasn't an A student anymore.

School had become a place I didn't want to be in. Even the classes I liked weren't fun anymore. SMS had started to seem too big, too impersonal. I wanted attention, but not the kind I was attracting from some of the other kids.

That's why I was so happy to be accepted at Riverbend as a full-scholarship student. Now I could leave SMS behind and all the bad memories with it.

But what about the good memories? I knew there were some. I went back into my daydream and pictured them.

Like the time I wrote a play for an English-class project. My teacher, Mr. Williams, said it was the best project in class. Plus, the play — it was called *The Early Years*, and it was about my family — was put on at the elementary school. It was a smash hit.

Then there was the time I won an award on Young Author's Day for best overall fiction, sixth grade. That was a huge thrill.

So was the time I was elected sixth-grade class secretary, and the time I helped our class raise enough money to help pay for a student lounge in the library. I hoped my classmates would remember me for that.

Instead, I'd probably go down in history as Spaz Girl.

Daydreaming about school was not pleasant. But at least it reminded me that going to River-bend was the right choice. It would be easy to say good-bye to SMS.

But what about leaving my friends?

That wasn't so simple.

CHAPTER 2

I remember how, before Jessi moved here, I used to wish for a best friend. Now I have one. In fact, I have a whole bunch of them. Jessi's my _best_ best friend, but if I'm counting best friends I have to count everyone else in the BSC.

It was a relief to turn my thoughts away from school and toward the BSC. The Baby-Sitters Club has been one of the best things in my life ever since I joined it. To tell you the truth, I don't know how I would have made it through the Spaz Girl episode without the support of my friends in the club.

Maybe I should explain what the club is and how it works. It's pretty simple. We're a group of seven responsible sitters who meet three times a week, on Monday, Wednesday, and Friday afternoons, from five-thirty until six. During those times, parents can call to arrange for a sitter and be certain of finding someone available. I know my parents think the BSC is the greatest thing since sliced bread (my mom said that once). I sit for my own family a lot, but if all my siblings are home it's better to have two sitters. (In fact, it's a BSC rule that we send two sitters to any job involving more than four kids.) My parents never have trouble lining up the help they need, since there are seven regular sitters in the club. We even have two associate members who help out when we're swamped. That's partly why we're so successful.

We're also successful because we're really good sitters. We're not just in it for the money. We love kids and love to do things with them.

We play games, plan special events, and host parties for our charges. We keep track — in our club record book — of allergies and food preferences, along with information such as client names and addresses. And in our club notebook, we each write up every job we go on. That means we're always up-to-date. If Charlotte Johanssen needs help studying for a big test, or if Jackie Rodowsky has a cold, we're aware of it. In Charlotte's case, we'd make sure to remember to spend some time brushing up on third-grade math. For Jackie, we'd remember to bring along a Kid-Kit. Kid-Kits are boxes stuffed with toys and games (mostly hand-me-downs), stickers, and markers. Each of us has one, and they're great for entertaining bored or sick kids.

As I imagined a BSC meeting in the near future — sometime after I had left Stoneybrook — I saw Kristy Thomas, our president, looking worried about my absence. Without me on hand, there might not be enough sitters to go around at busy times. Kristy and the other club members had decided not to replace me for now. At first that had hurt my feelings. Was I dispensable? Didn't it matter whether I was there? But my friends assured me that it was more a matter of not being able to find anyone to fill my shoes.

Still, I knew Kristy would probably worry

about having to turn down clients. That's just Kristy. She takes the BSC seriously. And she has reason to. After all, it was her idea. That's why she's president.

Kristy's a true idea factory and a born leader. She's outspoken and opinionated. She's on the short side, with brown hair and brown eyes and no sense of style whatsoever (her daily "uniform" consists of jeans and whatever turtleneck is on top of the stack in her drawer). But even if her appearance is low-key, she's a dynamo. I think it's partly because of the way she grew up.

Kristy's dad walked out on her family years ago, leaving Kristy and her three brothers (two older, one younger) in their mother's care. Everyone had to take responsibility for keeping the family running, and they pulled together and made the best of it. Kristy's mom is a strong woman who never gave up. Now she's happily remarried, to a great guy named Watson Brewer. Watson has two children of his own, a son and daughter who are both younger than Kristy. (They live part-time with Watson and part-time with their mom.) He also has major money. In fact, he's a millionaire. When he and Kristy's mom married, Kristy moved across town to live in Watson's mansion.

Soon after that, two more people moved in:

Emily Michelle, a Vietnamese orphan adopted by Kristy's mom and Watson, and Nannie, Kristy's extremely energetic grandmother. As you can imagine, it's a full house — even if you don't count the assorted pets running around the place.

You'd think Kristy would be busy enough keeping up with her family, but no. She also coaches a kids' softball team, runs the BSC, and stays involved with school activities. As I said, she's a dynamo.

Kristy's best friend, Mary Anne Spier, is the club's secretary. I closed my eyes and visualized Mary Anne. What would she be doing at a meeting after I'd gone?

I smiled.

"I miss Mallory so much," she'd say in her quiet voice. "How about if we send her a care package? You know, some cookies, a book, stuff like that."

That's Mary Anne. Shy, sensitive, and always a thoughtful friend. She and Kristy are very different; in fact, sometimes it seems that all they have in common is their looks. Mary Anne also has brown hair and brown eyes, and she's not particularly tall. She does dress a little more interestingly than Kristy, though.

Mary Anne grew up as an only child in a single-parent family. Her mom died a long time ago, when Mary Anne was just a baby. After her dad struggled through the worst of his grief, he turned his attention to bringing up Mary Anne. He paid her almost too much attention. He was overly strict and didn't seem to want to let her grow up.

Now he's much more easygoing. We all think that has to do with the fact that he's married again, to his high school sweetheart, no less. Her name is Sharon. She grew up in Stoneybrook, like Mary Anne's dad did. But she moved out to California, married, and had two kids. When the marriage ended, she came back to Stoneybrook, bringing the kids (Dawn, who's Mary Anne's age, and Jeff, who's younger) with her. Dawn and Mary Anne met and became best friends. Soon enough, their parents fell in love again and wedding bells rang.

Mary Anne was happy to be part of a bigger family. But Jeff had decided he was happier living in California, and then Dawn came to the same conclusion. So they both live with their dad. Dawn was a BSC member, and now she's an honorary member. She returns to Stoneybrook for vacations and holidays. I know Mary Anne misses her a lot. Even though Mary Anne has a steady boyfriend (Logan Bruno, one of our associate members) and an adorable kitten named Tigger, nothing is quite the same as a sister and best friend rolled into one.

Abby Stevenson would probably agree with that. She's the newest member of the BSC. She took over Dawn's old job, alternate officer. That means she fills in for any other officer who can't make a meeting.

I'd say Abby's twin sister, Anna, is the closest thing she has to a best friend. Abby and Anna have dark, curly hair and wear glasses (or contacts — I'm green with envy). But they're not carbon copies of each other. Abby is boisterous and full of fun. She's an athlete too, despite her asthma and allergies. Anna is quieter, and her love is the violin. She's always practicing, and it shows. I've never heard anyone her age play nearly as well.

Abby and Anna moved here only recently, when their mom was promoted at work (she's a high-powered editor at a big New York publishing house) and wanted to live in a new neighborhood. They used to live on Long Island. They were there when Mr. Stevenson died a few years ago in a car crash. That must have been horrible for them. Abby doesn't talk about him much, but when she does she gives the impression that he was a great dad. I think the girls were sad that he couldn't be present for their Bat Mitzvah, which is a ceremony that welcomes Jewish girls into adulthood.

Still daydreaming, I pictured Abby reading through the club notebook. She'd probably notice that there was a lot less to read now that I had left. (I was probably the only club member who actually enjoyed writing up my jobs.) I knew she'd also miss me as the perfect audience for her jokes. While other BSC members sometimes groaned at her terrible puns, I would always laugh.

In my daydream, everyone was laughing now. Not because of one of Abby's jokes, but because of something Claudia Kishi had said. Claudia's the club's vice-president. Meetings are held in her room because she happens to have her own phone — and a separate line. (She's so cool.) Anyway, I pictured her agreeing with Mary Anne's idea about sending a care package to me. "We can send her some of those gourmet jelly beans," she said. "And some Oreos, and some Pringles —"

Junk Food + Claudia = Love.

That's what cracked everybody up. Trust Claudia to see a box filled with cookies and candy as the best thing to send me.

She'd probably also want to throw in the latest Nancy Drew book. Claudia's a big fan of those mysteries. But, *shhh!* Don't tell her parents. They've forbidden junk food and junk reading (which is what they call Nancy Drew mysteries). They'd rather have her eating carrots and reading Dickens.

Claudia is Japanese-American, with long,

shiny black hair and beautiful dark eyes. And while her parents are strict, they're also very loving. They try hard to accept Claudia for what she is: an artistic genius. Claudia is the most talented artist at SMS. She draws, she paints, she sculpts, she makes her own jewelry . . . there's no limit to her creativity. She's also creative when it comes to her spelling — maybe a little too creative. School doesn't interest her much. In fact, she even had to spend some time repeating seventh grade not too long ago. Now she's back in eighth, but she's still dating a seventh-grader.

(I should mention here that all the BSC members except Jessi and me are thirteen and in the eighth grade. Like me, Jessi's eleven and in the sixth.)

Claudia's older sister, Janine, would never have to repeat a grade. She'd be more likely to skip one, since she's incredibly smart. She's in high school, but she's already taking college classes. But you know what? She can't draw at all.

Claudia's best friend is Stacey McGill. She's the treasurer of the BSC, and I pictured her frowning over the records she keeps. The BSC members pay dues each week and the money is used to cover club expenses such as Claudia's phone bill. If there's any extra, Stacey will declare that it's time for a pizza party. "Without Mal, there won't be too much left over this month," she would report. "Once we pay Claud's phone bill and cover Charlie's gas money, that is." Charlie is Kristy's older brother. He drives Kristy to meetings, along with Abby (who lives in Kristy's neighborhood) and, occasionally, Shannon Kilbourne (our other associate member, who also lives near Kristy).

I felt a little guilty when I pictured the treasury crisis — but not *that* guilty. After all, did I really want them to have a pizza party without me?

Back to Stacey. Stacey has blonde hair and sparkling blue eyes, and always looks classy and sophisticated. I think that kind of fashion sense comes naturally to anyone born on the island of Manhattan. Stacey is still a New Yorker at heart, even though she lives here in Stoneybrook with her mom. Her parents are divorced, and Stacey's dad lives in the Big Apple. She visits him whenever she can — and takes advantage of all the great shopping while she's there.

Figuring out how much she's spent is no hardship for Stacey. She's a math whiz. She's even on the SMS math team.

If it sounds as if life is easy for Stacey, you don't really know her. Stacey has diabetes, a serious, lifelong condition. Her system has trouble processing sugars, which means she has to be very careful about what she eats. She also has to test her blood for sugar content and give herself injections of insulin, which her body doesn't produce in the proper amount. Not fun. But Stacey handles it all very well. I've always admired her for that.

I pictured Stacey collecting dues from everyone. She passed around a manila envelope, and it went from hand to hand. First to Claudia, sitting next to Stacey on the bed. Then to Mary Anne, on the other side of Claud. Over to Abby, who was perched on a trunk at the foot of the bed. A toss from Abby to Kristy, sitting in a director's chair near Claudia's desk. And from Kristy to — Jessi, sitting alone on the floor.

Jessi. My best friend. How can I even begin to imagine how much we'll miss each other? She won't be able to help me through my first days at school. I won't be able to sit with her at BSC meetings, or eat lunch with her, or hang out with her after school and on weekends. I felt a lump grow in my throat as I pictured her.

Jessi has cocoa-colored skin and chocolate-brown eyes. She has long, strong legs and she holds herself with elegance and grace. That's because she's a dancer, a ballerina. She's been studying ballet for years and will probably dance professionally when she's older.

We clicked immediately when we met. We have a lot in common, especially our love for reading. We'd only been friends for a day before we began trading our favorite books. We're both nuts about horse stories.

Jessi's family is a lot smaller than mine. She has a younger sister named Becca, and a baby brother named Squirt — or John Philip Ramsey, Jr., if you want to be formal. Her parents both work, and Jessi's aunt Cecelia lives with the family too. She helps care for the younger kids.

Jessi. Would she find a new best friend after I left? (I didn't want her to be lonely, but how could she replace me?) Or would she throw herself into ballet?

No matter what, I knew she'd always be there for me. So would my other friends in the BSC. And I would always be there for them. I knew that for sure.

Enough daydreaming. The rest of my family just came home and it's time to join them downstairs. After all, I haven't left yet!

CHAPTER 3

"Order! I said, order!" Kristy was tapping a pencil on Claudia's desk. "Come on, you guys, how about a little order?"

"A little?" asked Abby. "We can handle that. As long as it's only a little." She stuck two fingers in her mouth and whistled loudly (she can do that even better than Kristy can).

We turned to look at her. It was Friday at precisely 5:34. The BSC members were gathered in Claudia's room for a meeting, a real one this time. But nobody seemed to be in the mood for business.

Stacey and Claudia were sampling nail polishes, giggling as they tried to decide which was truly the weirdest: a dark blue one with glitter or a bright orange one that looked like a highway sign. Jessi and I were sitting on the floor together, trying to figure out a secret code we could use for our letters and e-mail once I was at Riverbend. So far neither of us had been able to completely decipher the notes we'd composed for each other. "Meet me at the — *glormo*?" Jessi asked, puzzling over my note.

"Not the glormo," I said. "The corner. And what about your note, the one about what you had for dinner last night. What in the world is bugustu?"

"Lasagna!" shrieked Jessi, who was laughing so hard she had to roll around on the floor, holding her stomach. "Not bugustu, lasagna!"

Abby joined in. "Chocolate-flavored bugustu? Yum."

"Did somebody say chocolate?" interrupted Claudia. "Mary Anne, could you do me a favor? My nails aren't totally dry, so I can't grab it, but there's a bag of Kisses under my pillow." She held up her hands to show off her nails, which were painted in alternating blue and orange.

Mary Anne rummaged around beneath the pillow and came up with the Kisses. "Here they are!" she called, pulling them out. The bag was open, and the chocolates flew all over the room. "Oops! Sorry," said Mary Anne, as we all dove for them.

It was during that mad scramble that Kristy called for order a second time. We fell silent. I looked around the room at my friends. This was the kind of BSC meeting I was especially going to miss. Would I ever feel this comfortable with new friends?

Kristy looked back at us and grinned. "Okay, carry on," she said, picking up a Kiss and tossing it to me. "I just wanted to make sure I could get your attention if I needed it. I know this isn't going to be a regular meeting. After all, it's Mal's last one. Let's have fun."

"Woo! Madame President cuts loose!" teased Claudia.

Everybody started tossing Kisses and laughing again — everybody except me. The words "Mal's last one" played over and over in my mind. My last BSC meeting. Was this really the last time I'd sit in Claudia's room, surrounded by six best friends? I felt tears form in my eyes as I considered the thought.

"Mal? Are you okay?" Mary Anne slid off the bed and put her arm around me. Trust Mary Anne to notice that I wasn't exactly celebrating.

"It's just —" I began, feeling a tear run down my cheek, "it's just that I can't stand the idea that this is really my last BSC meeting ever."

The room fell silent. Suddenly everybody was looking at me.

"Who said that?" asked Kristy. "Nobody said that." She paused. "Or, at least, if I did say it, I didn't mean it." She glanced around at the others. "I think it's time," she said.

Mary Anne nodded.

"Time for what?" I asked, sniffling a little.

"Time for the ceremony," said Claudia, jumping up to rummage around in her desk drawer. (Her nails were obviously dry by now.) Kristy shoved her director's chair back to give Claudia room.

"Ceremony?" I repeated. "What ceremony?"

"The one at which we make you an Official —" Kristy began to announce. Then she interrupted herself. "Did you find it?" she asked Claudia.

"It's here somewhere." Claud stuck her hand deep into the bottom drawer and pulled something out. "Ta-da!" she said, holding it up. It looked like a certificate, decorated with stars and rainbows.

"An Official Honorary Member of the BSC," Kristy finished, as Claudia handed me the certificate. Everybody applauded and cheered. Mary Anne, who was still next to me on the floor, gave my shoulder a squeeze.

"For life, that is," Kristy added. "You're always welcome at meetings, Mal, and we hope you'll take sitting jobs when you come home for breaks."

Everybody cheered again.

"We mean that," Mary Anne said. "You're an important part of this club, and we're not ready to give you up completely."

Another tear escaped and ran down my cheek. Mary Anne was prepared. She handed me a tissue. "I had a feeling this might be an emotional moment," she said. She looked a little teary herself.

Kristy shook her head. "And to think that at first we almost didn't let you join the BSC," she said. "What were we thinking? We gave you that ridiculous test that nobody could have passed — "

"We even made you draw a picture of the digestive system!" hooted Claudia. "And then you came along on a job with me," she added, "as another test. But I made you so nervous that you dropped a glass of milk and let the dog in by mistake. I didn't give you a chance to prove what a good sitter you were."

"That's when we decided to start our own club," Jessi spoke up. "Kids Incorporated. Remember? We were just becoming best friends. Our club was good too."

"So good that Kristy couldn't stand the competition!" Stacey said. "She broke down and we asked Mal to join — "

"But you held out," said Jessi, smiling at me. "You said you wouldn't join unless I was invited too."

"And the rest is history," Kristy concluded.

"Wow," Abby said. "I don't think I ever heard this story before. That's great. So, what were some of your best moments as a BSC member?" she asked me.

Hmm. That was a tough question. So tough that for a few moments I couldn't think of a thing to say.

"Mal?" Abby asked.

"It's just that there are so many great memories," I said slowly. "I love all the kids we sit for, and we've had so much fun with them. I remember talent shows, and summer day camp, and circuses, and parades — not to mention the quiet times, just reading or talking or playing cards. And then there's all the cool stuff we've done as a club, like our trip to California, and our cruise, and our visit to Europe. Plus the pizza parties we've had, and the mysteries we've solved together. I mean, it's hard to pick the best out of all that."

"I'll tell you one of Mal's best moments as a sitter," Kristy volunteered. "It happened not that long after she joined the club."

I looked at Kristy, wondering what she had in mind.

She smiled at me. "It was when you figured out what was wrong with the Arnold twins," she said. "That was when I knew for sure that you were going to be a really valuable member of the BSC."

"That was great," agreed Mary Anne.

Stacey turned to Abby. "The twins had been

acting like spoiled brats," she explained. "And nobody could figure out why. Until Mallory had a brainstorm."

"It was just that they were tired of being treated like clones," I said, blushing a little. "They used to have the same haircut, the same room decor, the same outfits every day. They were sick of it! All they needed was a chance to express their individual personalities."

"They've been great ever since," Claudia added.

"I can't even imagine them dressing alike," said Abby. "That's awesome, Mal."

"It was no big deal," I answered. Secretly, though, I loved feeling so smart.

"I remember another charge you really helped," said Mary Anne. "Buddy Barrett. He was having trouble keeping up with his class in reading," she explained to Abby.

"That's right!" Stacey exclaimed. "And nobody could figure out how to help him. I remember Dawn tried really hard. But Mal was the one who found the key."

"Comic books!" I said, remembering. "He loved comics, so I thought, why not? We ended up writing our own comic books. Now he loves to read."

"You also helped the Delaneys," Stacey pointed out. "You know, back when your dad — " She stopped. "Sorry."

"That's okay," I said. "It wasn't a great time in my life, but it's over now." I turned to Abby. "My dad lost his job," I explained. "We were really worried about money, so I was doing a lot of sitting."

"And we had these clients, the Delaneys," Claudia told her. "Rich snobs."

"Claudia!" Mary Anne looked disapproving.

"Well, they were," said Claudia. "They lived where the Kormans live now, in that huge mansion with the fountain and the tennis courts and the pool. All the neighborhood kids used to go there just to swim. And even though the Delaney kids were rich snobs, it started to hurt their feelings. So Mal helped them figure out a way to find out who their real friends were."

"I was finding out who *my* real friends were then too," I murmured, remembering how nasty some of the kids at school had been, teasing me about my dad losing his job — and how great my BSC friends had been.

"You've had quite a sitting career," said Abby.

"Well, it hasn't all been wonderful," I answered. "I've been through plenty of food fights and barf cleanups and name-calling and broken bones too."

"And that's just with her own brothers and sisters," said Jessi, cracking up.

"We've been through all that and more just during one dinner at my house," I said.

"Speaking of which," said Claudia, cocking her head toward the clock. "Shouldn't we be finishing our meeting?"

It was six o'clock. Time for my last BSC meeting — that is, my last one as a regular member — to end.

"Yup. This meeting is officially over," Kristy declared. Then everyone stood up and stretched and started pulling on jackets. It was over — just like that.

"See you, everybody!" Abby called as she and Kristy headed out the door.

"But — " I wasn't ready for the meeting to end so quickly.

"Charlie's probably waiting downstairs," Kristy added. "Gotta go!" She waved.

Then Stacey left, saying she and her mom were going out for dinner. Mary Anne had to leave because she was expecting a phone call from Dawn. Soon just Jessi, Claud, and I were left. Jessi and I had planned to walk home together.

"Well — 'bye," I said to Claud.

"Hold on, Mal." She held up a hand. "I have something for you." She reached under her bed and pulled out a wrapped package. She handed it to me. "It's a going-away present."

I opened it to find a beautiful sketchbook

bound in black leather. "This is gorgeous. Thanks, Claud."

"It's for your drawings. So when you're a famous author-illustrator, you can show it to your fans and tell them about your early years."

I gave her a hug. "Thanks," I said again.

Jessi was waiting with her jacket on. "Ready?" she asked.

I nodded.

"I'll walk with you guys," Claudia offered. "It's Janine's turn to start dinner."

We walked along, talking about nothing much. I felt strange, knowing that twenty-four hours later I'd be far away from Stoneybrook and all my friends.

My house was the first stop, and Claudia and Jessi walked me up the steps to the front door. I opened it and turned to say good-bye. "SURPRISE!" I heard. I jumped, and turned again to see that my house was crammed with people.

My parents. My brothers and sisters. Every member of the BSC, even Logan and Shannon. And many of our regular charges. The Arnold twins, the Rodowsky boys, the Hobarts — including Ben (my sort-of boyfriend), who was holding a big bunch of flowers. Plus Charlotte Johanssen, Matt and Haley Braddock . . .

I felt my eyes fill with tears. "What is this?" I

asked. "I thought I already had my big day."

"That was just We Love Mallory Day," explained Jessi, who put her arm around my shoulders as we stood in the doorway. "This is your going-away party. And it's going to be a great one. We've been planning like crazy."

Just then, the crowd of people surged toward me, calling my name. I felt — everything. Thrilled. Sad. Happy.

Loved.

CHAPTER 4

I knew it before I even opened my eyes.

This was a big day.

It was *the* day, at last.

In a matter of hours I would be on my way to Riverbend Hall.

I yawned and stretched and then opened my eyes. I looked around the room. My familiar room, the one in which I'd spent nearly every night for eleven years. There was my bookshelf — with a few gaps in it. (I'd packed my favorite books to take with me.) There was my desk, where I'd slaved over so much homework. My poster showing the different breeds of horses. The yellow curtains I'd made with my mom's help. The big wooden "M" my dad had found at a junk shop.

My trunk and my suitcase were neatly packed and ready to go.

Wow. I was really leaving. I mean, obviously I knew that. I was the one who'd applied to the school and waited anxiously to hear if I'd been accepted. I was the one who'd agonized over whether to go once I'd been accepted. And I was the one who'd enjoyed every minute of the special attention my friends had been giving me: We Love Mallory Day, my honorary membership in the BSC, my most excellent surprise going-away party . . .

So of course I knew I was leaving.

But somehow I hadn't quite believed it. Until now. Suddenly, it all seemed very real. And very scary.

Maybe I'd made the wrong decision. Maybe this was crazy. Maybe I should stay. Maybe I'd be able to figure out some way to make myself fit in at SMS.

I took a deep breath. There I was, still lying in bed, working myself into a tizzy. I was being ridiculous. I knew that going away to River-bend was the right thing to do. After all, I'd thought it over for a good, long time. I was just nervous, which was understandable.

"Mal?" I heard a drowsy voice calling my name.

I turned to look over at the other side of the room, the side with a poster of Emily Dickinson over the bed. Vanessa's bed.

"Good morning, Vanessa," I said.

"Sunny or cloudy?" Vanessa asked.

I laughed. Vanessa has asked me that question just about every morning for years. She likes to know what to expect before she opens her eyes. "Sunny," I answered. "What are you going to do for a weather report once I'm gone?"

"I've already lined up Nicky," she said. "I'm paying him a nickel a week to come in here and tell me what kind of day it is."

I laughed again. "You mean I could have been charging you all this time?"

Vanessa laughed. Then she fell silent. "Mal?" she asked after a moment.

"Yes?"

"I'm really, really going to miss you."

"I'm going to miss you too." I sat up in bed. "But I'll be back for holidays and stuff, and I'll be here all summer."

"It won't be the same," said Vanessa.

"I know," I agreed. "It won't." She was right. Nothing would ever be quite the same. But that didn't have to be a bad thing.

"Now, how about my morning poem?" I asked. In exchange for my weather report, Vanessa has made up a little poem for me each day.

Vanessa rolled over and groaned. "I wanted to make you a really special one," she said. "But then we went to that movie, and there was the party and I didn't have time."

"It doesn't matter," I told her. "Just a short one will be fine."

Vanessa thought for a minute. "Okay, here goes," she said. "Today's the day!/It's super cool./Mallory's going off to school."

I applauded. Vanessa jumped out of bed and took an enormous bow.

"Thank you so much, ladies and gentlemen," she said. "Thank you, thank you."

"Girls!" That was my mom's voice from downstairs. "Vanessa, Mallory! Are you almost ready to join us for breakfast?"

"Coming!" I called. I hopped out of bed and looked for my bathrobe. Oops. It was already packed. I decided to head downstairs in my pajamas.

"There she is," my dad said as I entered the kitchen. He was busy at the stove, flipping pancakes.

"It's about time," grumbled Adam. "Mom said we had to wait for you this morning. I'm starving!"

"Don't listen to him," my mom said, giving me a hug. "The pancakes weren't ready yet anyway. Did you sleep well?"

"Uh-huh," I replied. It was true, I had. I guess I'd been too tired to let nervousness keep me awake.

I took my place at the table and looked around at my family as we ate breakfast together for the last time. (Or at least the last time for awhile.) The scene was as chaotic as ever, but I didn't let the noise, the syrup-spilling, and the squabbles over who'd had more pancakes bother me. That was my family, and I loved them just the way they were. I was lucky, really lucky to have such a great family. And no matter what, I knew I'd always be a part of them, and they'd be a part of me.

I gazed down at the last bite of my pancake without seeing it. My eyes smarted and I had a lump in my throat.

"Are you okay, Mal?" my mom asked gently.

I nodded. "I'm just going to miss everybody a lot."

"You won't if we never get you off to school," my dad observed, pushing back his chair and picking up his empty plate. "I think it's about time we loaded up the car." He patted the top of my head as he passed me on his way to the kitchen. "Better put some clothes on, kiddo," he said. "Unless you're planning to meet all your new friends dressed like that."

I looked down at my pajamas and laughed. The lump disappeared from my throat and my eyes stopped hurting. "Nope," I said. "I know exactly what I'm going to wear. My jeans and the blue sweater you and Mom gave me for Christmas." I'd planned that already, knowing I wanted to look good and feel comfortable.

Back upstairs, I took one last look around the room as I pulled on my clothes. Was there anything I'd forgotten to pack? As I checked my bookshelf one more time, I heard footsteps on the stairs. Footsteps I recognized, because they belonged to my best friend. I ran to the door and threw it open. "Hey, Jessi," I said.

"Hey," she answered. "I can't believe you're really leaving today." She looked sad — but also excited. "I bet you're going to love it there, Mal. You're going to make so many new friends."

"I hope so. But no matter how many friends I make, you'll always be my best friend."

We hugged.

"We'll write letters," she promised. "And call."

"Don't forget e-mail," I reminded her. "You have my address, right?" Riverbend had e-mail, and each student had a private address. I'd received mine in an information packet. I'd made everyone in the BSC promise to keep me updated on our clients and any other Stoneybrook news.

"Right. Hey, you look great," she said, stepping back to check my outfit.

"Thanks. Want to help me lug this trunk downstairs?"

Together we lifted it and maneuvered our way into the hall. By the time we made our way down the stairs and out the front door, my dad had pulled the car out of the garage. It was sitting by the curb, the engine running.

"You two are strong," he said. "Good job." He took the trunk and lifted it into the back of the station wagon.

I ran back to the house to grab the little suitcase. When I lugged it outside I found my family gathered around the car. Plus, Mary Anne had arrived. She'd be helping Jessi sit for my brothers and sisters while my parents drove me to school.

Before I knew it, the car was loaded. Suddenly, everything was happening too fast.

"Say good-bye, everybody," my dad said. He checked his watch. "We need to head out."

One by one, my sisters and brothers stepped up to me. Even the triplets let me hug them, which is rare. Then Mary Anne hugged me. Then Jessi. Then it was time to go.

I stepped into the car and closed the door.

"Ready?" my dad asked.

I looked out the window at my family and friends. My face felt wet, and I realized that I was crying.

"Ready," I answered.

CHAPTER 5

Saturday

Uh-oh. Trouble at the O.K. Corral.

No kidding. Maybe Mal's presence was the secret to keeping the Pike family in balance.

That's a scary thought. After all, will be the ones sitting for them from now on. It was always a challenge, even when Mal was around. But now?

Challenge plus.

Maybe things will settle down soon.

Maybe so. But I have a feeling that the situation will get worse before it gets better.

Jessi and Mary Anne were in agreement. A storm was brewing at the Pike house, and it was a big one. The first clouds rolled in only minutes after my parents and I had driven off. (I heard about it when Jessi sent me a long e-mail.)

Mary Anne and Jessi were talking together quietly, consoling each other after my departure, when they heard a fight begin in the hallway.

"Where do you think you're going?" Adam demanded as Margo started up the stairs.

"To my room," Margo answered. She looked very unhappy. Losing her big sister was not going to be easy for her.

"You haven't finished cleaning up the kitchen yet," Adam said, arms folded across his chest.

("Like the Pike family cop," Jessi told me.)

"But it's not my turn," Margo replied. "I did it last night." She was on the brink of tears.

"That's not the point. Now that Mal's gone, we're all going to have to pitch in more. And you're going to have to listen to what I tell you."

"Why?" Margo asked defiantly.

"Because I'm the oldest now." Adam looked triumphant.

"Actually, *I'm* the oldest," Jordan pointed out.

He elbowed Adam aside. "I was born first, re-member?"

"Oh, big deal," said Adam. "We're all ten, that's the main point. The oldest kids in the family, now that Mallory is away."

"Right, we're oldest," Jordan agreed. "It's our job to be in charge when Mom and Dad are gone. We're in charge of all the little kids, and I'm in charge of you two."

"Forget *that*!" Adam cried. "Nobody's in charge of me."

"Me neither," Byron agreed. "I can take care of myself."

By this time, Margo had seen her chance and headed up the stairs, leaving the triplets to ar-gue among themselves.

Jessi and Mary Anne approached the boys. Adam's fists were clenched. The fight was about to turn physical.

"Hold on, hold on," said Jessi. "Let me point out that the only ones in charge here are Mary Anne and me."

At one time, the triplets had insisted that they were too old to need sitters anymore. In fact, they'd even experimented with being ju-nior sitters. But the experiment hadn't worked out. Now the BSC members sit for my big family, triplets and all, sending two sitters if all the kids are at home. We try not to order the triplets around, but sometimes they just *ask* for it. This was one of those times.

"And we'd like you boys to finish cleaning up the kitchen," Mary Anne added sweetly.

"See what you did?" Jordan whispered furiously to Adam.

"It wasn't *my* fault."

Byron frowned at both of them and the boys clammed up and marched into the kitchen.

"Yesss!"

Jessi and Mary Anne whirled around to see Nicky, who'd been hiding in a little crawl space beneath the stairs.

"Thank you, thank you, thank you," he said. "I just knew Jordan was going to start being bossy as soon as he had the chance." He did a little dance. "Now nobody's going to be bossing me around."

"Ahem," said Jessi. "Except us. I believe your mom mentioned something about picking up your Legos? The ones that are about to take over the entire living room?"

Nicky frowned. "Mal wouldn't have made me take apart my castle."

"But we're not Mal," Mary Anne pointed out.

"That's for sure," mumbled Nicky as he slouched off toward the living room.

Jessi and Mary Anne looked at each other

and shrugged. It seemed as if all the Pike kids were going to be cranky that day.

But they hadn't seen anything yet.

They headed upstairs to see what the girls were doing — and found Claire lying in the hall, crying her heart out.

"Claire!" Jessi exclaimed.

"What's the matter?" Mary Anne asked, dropping to her knees. "Did you hurt yourself?"

"N-No," sobbed Claire. "I just miss Mallory."

"Of course you do — " Mary Anne began to say.

"And M-M-Mommy and Daddy," Claire added. "Why do they want to go live in Chassamoosets anyway?" She hiccuped and wept some more.

Mary Anne and Jessi exchanged a puzzled look.

"Do you mean Massachusetts?" Jessi asked.

Claire nodded, still sobbing.

"But your parents aren't going to live there," Mary Anne explained. "They're just driving Mallory to her new school. They'll be back tonight."

"They will?" Claire looked up and sniffed. "But I thought — "

"You thought your parents were going away too? Well, they're not. And Mallory isn't going away forever. She'll be back for vacations and for the summer. It's only boarding school."

Claire sat up and rubbed her eyes.

"And you can write letters to her and call her," Jessi added. "And she'll write you back."

"I can't write so well yet," admitted Claire.

"You can send her a picture," Mary Anne said. "In fact, how about starting one right now? We can send it to her today. I bet it will cheer her up. I'm sure she's going to miss you too."

Claire was looking much happier. "And Mom and Dad will be home tonight?" she asked again.

"In time for dinner," Mary Anne promised. She and Jessi helped Claire up and walked with her into the room she shares with Margo. Margo was already at work at her desk, on — guess what? — a letter to me.

"Does she have to come in here right now?" Margo complained. "I'm trying to concentrate."

"Claire won't bother you," Mary Anne promised.

"Ha!" said Margo. "You never had to live with her. In about three seconds she'll be singing silly songs. Wait and see!"

Claire stuck out her lower lip. "Will not," she answered. "I'll be quiet. I just want to work on a picture for Mallory."

Jessi helped Claire settle in at her desk, setting her up with paper and crayons. "There you go," she said. She and Mary Anne headed out, only to hear Claire start in on "The Wheels on the Bus" before they'd even reached the stairs.

"Aaugh!" they heard Margo cry.

"Claire," Jessi called warningly. The song stopped for a second, then started up much more quietly. Jessi and Mary Anne smiled at each other.

Then Mary Anne suggested that they check on Vanessa. They knocked on the door of the room she'd shared with me. "Come in," called Vanessa in a sad voice.

The room was dark and quiet. The shades were down and the curtains were drawn. Vanessa sat at her desk, bent over a notebook lit by a pool of light from a small lamp. She was dressed in black from head to foot and looked like a romantic heroine wasting away from sorrow.

"It's so tragic," she said in a hollow voice. "Mallory was the world to me."

"She's not — she's not *dead*," Mary Anne pointed out.

Vanessa sighed. "I didn't think you'd understand. After all, you've never lost a dear sister."

"Actually, I have —" began Mary Anne, thinking of how much it had hurt when Dawn moved back to California.

But Vanessa interrupted her. "I've been working on some poems about it," she said. "Would you like to hear them?" She picked up a sheaf of paper and started to read from the top sheet. " 'It was a sad winter's day, when you went away,' " she began.

"I think I hear the triplets fighting again," Jessi said, cocking her head. "We'd better check on them."

Mary Anne could hear the triplets too. "We'll listen to your poems later," she told Vanessa.

They escaped down the hall. "Wait until Mallory hears how much everyone misses her," Jessi said to Mary Anne.

They reached the bottom of the stairs, only to find the triplets, Nicky, Claire, and Margo waiting for them. The kids stood with hands on hips, frowning.

"What's up, guys?" asked Jessi.

"Where were you?" demanded Jordan.

"Upstairs," answered Mary Anne, bewildered. Why was everybody glaring at them? "In Mal — I mean, in Vanessa's room."

"See?" asked Jordan, turning to face the others. "I told you. It's already been decided, and we had no say."

"What's been decided?" Jessi asked, just as confused as Mary Anne.

"That I'm going to keep that room all to myself," said Vanessa, who had appeared on the stairs behind them. "That's what you're all worried about, isn't it?" she called down to her brothers and sisters. "You're hoping for a chance at that room. Well, you can forget about it. I've waited all my life for a room of my own, and now I'm going to have it."

The other kids erupted into shouts.

Mary Anne and Jessi looked at each other helplessly. They'd thought things were bad already — but they had only seen the tip of the iceberg.

The Pike Room Wars were about to begin.

CHAPTER 6

" 'Bye, Mom. 'Bye, Dad. Thanks for everything. I'll call you soon."

This was it. My parents were leaving, and my life at Riverbend was about to begin. Part of me felt terrified, like a kindergartner saying good-bye to her mommy on the first day of school. But most of me felt excited.

I admit I was a little choked up as I hugged Mom and Dad good-bye. But I wasn't going to make a scene. My parents had helped me move into my room at Riverbend, and now it was time for them to head home to my brothers and sisters. And I had an orientation to attend.

By myself.

Anyway, let me back up and tell you about my arrival. Riverbend Hall is on the outskirts of a little town called Easton, which is about twenty miles away from Stockbridge, one of the bigger cities in this part of Massachusetts. The area is known as the Berkshires, after the mountain range that runs through it. As you can probably imagine, it's very pretty, even in the middle of winter. Country roads, trees, rolling hills — you get the picture.

We stopped for lunch in Easton, at a little luncheonette called Anita's. The waitress was very friendly and asked me if I was going to Riverbend. I was too nervous to chat much with her and way too nervous to enjoy my tuna-melt sandwich.

After lunch, we climbed into the car again and drove to Riverbend. I'd been there once before, also with my parents, when I visited in November. But this time was different. As we pulled off the main road and onto the smaller road that threads through the campus, I felt my heart beating faster. This wasn't just a visit. I wouldn't be in the car when my parents headed back to Stoneybrook. This was going to be my home.

Riverbend is a pretty place. It doesn't look anything like the schools in Stoneybrook. Instead of one huge building filled with classrooms, it's made up of a collection of smaller buildings. They look like houses, painted white with dark green shutters. Some contain offices, others are for classes, and some are dorms. There's also a library, a huge old red barn where art classes take place, and a sprawling brick meetinghouse where everybody eats their meals and where schoolwide meetings are held. All the buildings are connected by winding paths. There are open fields as well as areas with lots of trees, and a stream runs through the campus.

For the eightieth time I checked the letter I'd received from the admissions department. "My dorm is the third building on the right," I said. "It's called Earhart."

All the buildings at Riverbend are named after famous women. I liked the idea that my dorm was named after one of the pioneers of flight, Amelia Earhart.

"Earhart it is!" called out my dad. "I think I see it now." He parked the car and we piled out.

"It looks very homey," my mom said, putting her arm around me. "It even has the same kind of shutters as our house."

I nodded, although at that moment I wasn't sure familiar shutters were going to be enough to make me feel at home.

"Mallory Pike!" A tall girl with a long black braid had come out of Earhart's front door, and now she was striding toward me with her arms wide open. "I knew you'd be here any minute. Wonderful! Welcome to Riverbend. I'm Pam, your prefect. I'm a senior, but I live in the sixth-grade dorm as kind of a housemother." She gave me a quick hug. "And you must be Mrs.

and Mr. Pike. Come on in. Can I grab a suitcase or something?"

She was so full of smiles and enthusiasm that I forgot to be shy. "We can carry everything," I told her, "if you'll just show me where my room is."

"Okay," she said. "Follow me!" We grabbed my stuff out of the car and followed her into the house and up the stairs.

"This is it," she announced, throwing open a door. "Room nine. Of course, your roommate is already all moved in, because she's been here since September. But Alexis won't be back until tomorrow, along with the other students. Only you brand-new girls are arriving today. That should give you plenty of time to move in."

"Alexis?" I replied.

Pam nodded. "Alexis DeCamp. That's your roommate's name. She's — she's looking forward to meeting you, I'm sure."

For the first time, Pam didn't *sound* sure. But maybe that was my imagination.

"And now I have to fly. I have a meeting with my sculpture teacher. So make yourself at home. The bathroom's down the hall — I'm sure you'll find it — and there's a living room downstairs. You have orientation in a couple of hours, over at the meetinghouse. I'll see you after that."

With one last smile and a big wave, she was off.

My parents and I looked around the room, trying to figure out where to put all the things I'd brought. "There doesn't seem to be much space left," my father observed.

He was right. It wasn't a big room, and it seemed as if Alexis had claimed most of it. The room was square with white walls and woodwork. There were two beds, one on either side of the room, and two desks, one at the foot of each bed. Between two windows ran a long, low dresser with three big drawers on either side. There was a small closet as well.

One of the beds was bare; that was obviously mine. The other was covered with a vivid purple spread made of crushed velvet. The top of the dresser, which we were obviously meant to share, was covered with Alexis's things: perfume and makeup bottles and photos in silver frames. I wondered if she'd left me any drawer space and was relieved when I opened the top drawer on "my" side and saw that it was empty. Well, mostly empty. Except for three mismatched socks.

The closet was pretty full. That wasn't a big problem, since I hadn't brought too many clothes. I hung up a few things and put the rest, neatly folded, into my bottom drawer.

I looked around for a spot to hang up the

collage my friends had given me, which was made up of pictures of everyone in the BSC as well as of our charges. But Alexis had already hung up several posters — mostly of slightly scary-looking rock stars — and there didn't seem to be a bare spot big enough for my collage. I slid it under my bed to keep it safe until I could make room for it.

Mom helped me make my bed. My navy blue bedspread looked kind of boring next to Alexis's purple one, but I didn't care. It was familiar, and I was going to need all the help I could get to feel at home in this room.

We arranged my books on the desk nearest my bed, and I set my small collection of crystal horses on the windowsill next to the desk, not wanting to move Alexis's things from my half of the dresser top. She'd move them herself when she came back. I figured she must have left in a hurry for vacation, forgetting that she'd have a new roommate when she returned.

It didn't take long to unpack my stuff. Still, by the time we were done, it was almost time for orientation.

"Would you like us to walk you over there before we go?" asked Mom.

I shook my head. "No, I think I want to go alone." It was time to begin my new life, and I couldn't do that with my parents holding my hand.

My dad smiled. "Mal, we want you to know how proud we are of you. This is a big step for you, and you made the decision all by yourself. You're really growing up."

Oh, man. That lump in my throat? It was suddenly the size of Nebraska. I couldn't say a thing. I just hugged him. Then I hugged my mom. Then I said good-bye to them and let them walk out the door.

Without throwing myself at their legs.

After they'd gone, I looked around the room. Now that my stuff was unpacked, it looked a teensy bit more familiar. I lay down on the bed for a second, and stuck my nose into my pillow. It was the one from my bed at home, and I hope this doesn't sound too weird, but smelling it made me feel calm and peaceful. Somehow it reminded me that I was still me, Mallory Pike. Even though I was in a brand-new place where I didn't know anyone, I still had myself. Weird? I don't care.

I had one last thing to unpack: my journal. I pulled it out of my backpack and stuck it under my mattress.

Then I stood up and checked myself in the mirror on the inside of the closet door. Yup, I was still Mallory. Curls, glasses, braces, and all. Oh, well.

I headed for orientation.

There weren't many of us in the big meeting

hall. In fact, there was only one other new sixth-grader. I learned her name when Ms. Maxwell, the dean of students, asked us to introduce ourselves.

Smita Narula.

Now that's a much more interesting name than Mallory Pike. Smita looked beautiful, with her shiny black hair, black eyes, and light brown skin. She was Indian, she explained. Her parents had come to America the year before she was born. They used to live in New Delhi, and now they lived in New York City. Smita already had some friends who attended Riverbend, which is how she'd heard about it. I liked her right away. Her serene way of speaking made me feel calm and relaxed.

Smita and I sat together during Ms. Maxwell's presentation about Riverbend. I'd already heard most of the information during my visit last fall, but it was good to hear it again.

Riverbend is a special place. It's an alternative school with progressive ideas about education. The focus is on drama, writing, dance, visual arts, and music. Even the other courses such as math and gym are given a creative twist. Ms. Maxwell said we were expected to call our teachers by their first names, which I knew was going to be hard for me at first. (Ms.

Maxwell told us to call her Jane.) The youngest students are in fifth grade, the eldest in twelfth. Everybody lives in the dorms, and every dorm has a prefect.

Riverbend is collectively run, which means that all the students and teachers work to keep the school community going. Jobs are assigned on a monthly basis, and they include things such as yardwork, helping in the library, or working in the faculty day care center (yes!). As new students, we wouldn't be expected to help out until we'd settled in, so our jobs wouldn't start for a few weeks. Riverbend students and teachers also work in the larger community, doing volunteer projects in Easton and other local towns.

We met with Ms. Maxwell — Jane! — for about an hour. Then we sat down to a dinner of steak and salad (and pasta for any girls who were vegetarian). After that, orientation was over. Smita and I had discovered that we both lived in Earhart (she lives on the first floor), so we walked back to our dorm together.

Pam greeted us and showed us in to the living room. We sat and talked for awhile, but before long I realized that I was too tired to keep my eyes open. It had been a long day. I said good night to Pam and Smita and headed upstairs to bed. I was so sleepy I didn't even take time to write in my journal. I'd catch up the next day, which would be my first full day at Riverbend. As I drifted off to sleep, I crossed my fingers and hoped that it would be a good one.

CHAPTER 7

"Who are you?"

That was a tough question. Not only did I not know *who* I was, I didn't know where I was, or why I was there.

Did you ever wake up that way, on your first morning in a new place? Nothing seems familiar, and just for a second you feel lost in space. Then, after a moment, you start to put all the pieces back together.

"I'm Mallory," I answered groggily.

Mallory Pike. Waking to face my first day as a member of the Riverbend Hall community. And this girl standing over me must be my new roommate.

"Alexis?" I asked.

"Well, duh."

Oh, great. That was a good start.

"Are your parents here?" I asked.

"No. They just left."

"Oh." So it was just the two of us. Alone. For the next five months.

Suddenly, having a roommate seemed a little scary. I hadn't given it much thought; after all, I'd spent practically my whole life with a roommate. I was used to it. But a younger sister was one thing, and Alexis was another.

I sat up in bed, put on my glasses, and took a good look at Alexis DeCamp. My first impression? She was intimidating. She looked very mature, very sure of herself. Her blonde hair was cut short and spiked with gel. (I didn't know a single sixth-grader back in Stoneybrook with the guts for that kind of cut.) She wore a black sweater, a short black skirt, and black high-tops. No wishy-washy navy blue for this girl. Her jewelry? Well, I bet you can guess she wasn't wearing unicorn earrings or a smiley-face ring. No, she wore tiny black metal hoops, three in one ear, two in the other.

I looked down at my flowered flannel pajamas, feeling about six years old.

And I felt a knot begin to grow in my stomach.

What if I'd made a terrible mistake? What if the girls at Riverbend were just like the kids at SMS? What if — what if they were even worse? Maybe I wasn't going to fit in at all.

I tried to keep from panicking. I reminded myself about Smita and Pam and the other girls at orientation who had all seemed friendly and pleasant. I took a deep breath and tried to relax.

"So, here's the deal," Alexis announced as I got ready for brunch. "I've been at Riverbend for a year and a half now, and believe me, I know the ropes. Pay attention to what I tell you and you'll fit in just fine."

It was as if she'd read my mind. How could she know I was worried about fitting in?

"And as for our room, well, there are just a few basic rules. Rules that make life easier for everyone." Alexis began to pace around the room. She didn't seem to notice that I hadn't said a word since "Oh."

"First of all," she said, "we crack the window at night. It's healthier to have fresh air while you sleep."

I nodded, thinking I was going to have to ask my mom to send a heavier blanket.

"Quiet time is from four until six, after classes and before dinner. That's the best time to study."

I usually concentrate better after dinner, but I supposed I could adjust.

"I see you've taken over the windowsill for your stuff; that's fine," Alexis continued. "In that case I'll keep my things on the dresser. If you need more space, you can use the other windowsill too."

I opened my mouth, ready to say something about how little space two windowsills equaled, compared to that whole dresser top — but then I closed it. Was it really worth arguing over?

"It looks as if you don't need much closet space," Alexis observed, "which is great, because I don't know how I could spare it."

Yeesh. Okay, so I'll keep things in my drawers. As I said, I didn't bring many clothes.

"That's about it," Alexis said. "If anything else comes up I'm sure we can work it out."

Right. It wasn't taking me long to get the Alexis picture. *Kristy*, I thought to myself, *forgive me for ever thinking you were bossy. I didn't know what bossy was.*

Just then, there was a rapping on the door and Pam stuck her head in the room. "Oh, great," she said, smiling. "I see you two have met. Excellent. By the time you're up and done with all your unpacking, it will be time for Sunday brunch in the meetinghouse. See you there?"

"Sounds terrific," I said.

"Brunch." Alexis groaned. *"Fabulous."*

I think she was being sarcastic.

Pam didn't seem to notice. She just waved and headed off down the hall.

After she'd left, Alexis began to unpack her suitcase. She didn't seem to want to talk anymore. I decided it was a good time to catch up on my journal, so I reached under my mattress and pulled it out.

"What's that?" Alexis asked as soon as I'd started writing.

"Just a journal," I answered.

"Oooh, you mean where you write down all your most private and innermost thoughts?"

"Kind of." I shrugged.

"Aren't you worried someone will steal it and read it?"

"I never have been," I said, thinking I'd have to consider a new hiding place. "It's not like there are any big secrets in it." That wasn't exactly true. I was always honest in my journal, and that meant that what I wrote wasn't meant for other eyes.

Alexis continued to unpack, and I continued to write. But I couldn't help noticing that she kept sneaking glances at my journal. I wasn't used to that kind of interest. Vanessa had always seemed to understand that my journal was private. I guess I'd taken that kind of consideration for granted.

Suddenly, I heard a scuffling in the hall and a burst of giggles. "Knock, knock!" someone called out.

I recognized Smita's voice.

"Smita?" I called. "Come in." I stuck my journal back under the mattress.

"Not just Smita," said another voice. "Presenting . . . Sarah!" The two girls swept into the room. Smita, led by the other girl, was giggling and blushing. "You already know Smee, but you don't know me," the girl announced. "Sarah Bernhardt, at your service." She took a deep bow.

"Smee?" Alexis repeated snidely.

"That's what Sarah calls me," Smita explained. "Like the pirate in — "

"Peter Pan," Alexis finished. "Right. Cute."

I was still staring at Sarah. She was quite a presence. She was tall, for one thing, almost as tall as Kristy's brother Sam. She was dressed in flowing purple clothes — a long skirt and a silky shirt that seemed to shimmer when she moved. And she had a halo of flaming red hair, in wild ringlets. Her skin was pale with not one freckle. (How did she *do* that?) "Sarah Bernhardt?" I asked. "Like the famous actress?" I'd read about her. She was a French woman who became the most famous stage actress of her time (the late 1800s).

"Two points!" Sarah cheered. "Not everybody recognizes the name. But yes, I am named after La Bernhardt. And that means I have quite a reputation to live up to. Not that it's any trouble." She cracked up. "I *live* for the theatah," she said in a fake British accent.

There was something immediately likable about Sarah. Some people might be put off by her dramatic flair, but I loved it. I immediately began to imagine what her childhood had been like. No doubt she was the child of two actors who had led an incredibly romantic life barnstorming around the country.

"Sarah lives on your floor," Smita explained. "I just stopped up to visit her. We know each other from our old school."

"And now we're off to brunch," Sarah said. "Join us?"

I noticed that the invitation was aimed mostly in my direction. I figured Sarah and Alexis already knew each other, but I didn't sense any friendship there.

"I'd love to," I said. I was flattered. After all, both Smita and Sarah had other friends at Riverbend. They didn't have to include me. It felt great to be welcomed. "Um, Alexis, are you coming?" I asked, feeling a little awkward.

"I'm not hungry," she said flatly.

Oh. "Okay. See you at assembly, then?"

"Wouldn't miss it for the world." Alexis yawned, as if to show how much the idea bored her.

An assembly was scheduled for later that afternoon, the first one of the semester. I was looking forward to it. It would be my first chance to meet the whole Riverbend community.

The day went by in a blur. At brunch, Sarah and Smita introduced me to at least a dozen girls, but their names became jumbled in my head. The food was awesome: stacks of pancakes, homemade muffins, and fresh-squeezed juice. We ate and talked and ate some more, until we could barely move. I found out that instead of being the child of actors, Sarah is from the Midwest and her parents are teachers. When we finished eating, Smita suggested a walk. The three of us strolled around together, Sarah playing tour guide as she showed us the school.

Walking around the campus was like taking an introductory course in women's history. Sarah pointed out several other dorms: Stanton, named after the women's suffragist Elizabeth Cady Stanton; Truth, named after the abolitionist Sojourner Truth; and Jordan, named after the politician Barbara Jordan. Then there was the art building, which was known as O'Keeffe, after the famous artist Georgia O'Keeffe, and the science building (Curie, of course), and finally, the drama building.

"Someday it'll be named after me," Sarah vowed, striking a pose in front of the building, which is now known as Katharine Hepburn Hall.

I couldn't help thinking that she was probably right.

Our tour ended back at the meetinghouse, where the assembly was just about to start. Girls were streaming into the building, girls of every age and type, from childish-looking fifth-graders to seniors who looked like grown-up women. It was going to be interesting being in the same school as twelfth-graders. I spotted Alexis and waved to her, but she either didn't see me or pretended not to. Pam passed by and smiled at me.

Sarah, Smita, and I took seats near the front. I didn't want to miss a thing. Once again, Jane Maxwell stood up to talk. Then several teachers took turns talking about special projects they'd planned for the semester. Every speaker was full of enthusiasm; they were so inspiring. Finally, Jane Maxwell asked me and the other new girls to stand as we were introduced to the community. I was blushing like mad, but the loud, welcoming applause made me feel warm and accepted.

As we headed back to Earhart after the assembly, Sarah and Smita and I talked excitedly about the classes that would start the next day. I was feeling more positive by the moment that my choice to come to Riverbend had been the right one.

Then I walked back into my room.

"I thought we discussed the issue of shoes," Alexis said. No *Hello*, no *How did you like the assembly*.

"What?" I asked.

"Shoes. We take our shoes off when we come into the room," Alexis said slowly, as if she were talking to a child. She pointed to a small doormat where she'd left her boots. "Keeps the room cleaner. I thought you agreed."

"I don't even remember — " I began. Then I closed my mouth and slipped off my shoes. Something told me there was no point in arguing with Alexis.

I felt great about Riverbend, and I wasn't going to let Alexis ruin things for me. But how was I going to spend the next five months with her?

CHAPTER 8

"Ready for your first day of classes?" Alexis asked me the next morning.

"Definitely," I answered. She and I had woken early, with the sun streaming in through our windows. Alexis seemed to be in a much better mood. Maybe she'd just needed time to get used to the idea of having a new roomie.

"I bet you're going to love it here. I may not adore everything about this school, but I have to admit that the teachers are excellent." She hummed as she opened and closed her drawers, picking out an orange sweater and a pair of black jeans.

So that was it. She was in a good mood because she enjoyed going to class. That was interesting. Maybe we did have something in common after all. It felt great to be in a place where kids my age could feel so enthusiastic about learning, instead of making fun of people for being "brains." Great — and a little scary. Would I be smart enough to keep up?

"Who's your favorite teacher?" I asked.

"Ms. Orr," she answered immediately. "Kerry. The French teacher. She is totally cool."

I checked my schedule. "I have French at ten," I said. "Am I in your class?"

She shook her head. "No, I have it in the afternoon." She looked at my schedule. "But I'll see you in global studies, and it looks as if I'm in your English class too."

"Excellent," I said. I meant it too. I was beginning to think we might actually be able to become friends.

"Hey, you know what you'd look great in?" Alexis was back at the bureau, rummaging through the drawers. She pulled out a lime-green turtleneck sweater and tossed it to me. "Try this on."

"Um, actually, I already had an outfit picked out. Thanks, though," I said.

"Whatever." Alexis shrugged. "Just thought you might want to look a little more interesting."

Translation: Alexis thought my navy blue sweater was boring.

After a quick breakfast in the meetinghouse, I met up with Smita and headed for math class. "I'm so glad you're in my first class," I told her. "I'm a little nervous."

"Me too," she admitted. "But I hear our teacher is really nice."

Smita was right. Our math teacher was terrific. The class was unlike any I'd ever been in, but it didn't take me long to adjust.

First of all, there were only six girls in the class. We sat in a semicircle in a peaceful, sunlit room while Amy — that was my teacher's name, Amy Condon — explained what we'd be learning this semester. She seemed to love math so much that she made me excited about it too. We weren't going to spend the whole time staring at a blackboard, according to Amy. She'd be introducing us to ways math could be used in everyday life, so we'd be doing things like baking muffins for the whole school, taking surveys and putting together the results, and visiting the bank in downtown Easton.

After she'd talked for awhile, we went around the circle and introduced ourselves. We'd be working together throughout the semester, she explained, so we should start to become acquainted. I knew she did that for Smita's and my benefit, since the others already knew one another, and I appreciated it.

I think it was the first time I'd sat through an entire math class without feeling lost, anxious, or bored.

I *did* feel lost in French, my next class, but

somehow it didn't matter. I guess sometimes it can be fun to be lost. French class was definitely going to be an adventure.

Why?

Because right off the bat we were speaking only in French. "Entering *La Zone Française*. No English allowed in this room," the sign said on the door. I gulped and turned the knob. *"Bonjour!"* sang out the teacher. *"Je suis Kerry. Bienvenu!"*

Kerry was great. She made me feel comfortable right away, even though I didn't know any of the other girls in the class.

Now, I'd taken only a little French until then. But guess what? By the end of that day's class I was chatting away. I could even sing the words to *La Marseillaise*, which is the French national anthem. *Trés bien, non?*

Global studies was next. This was a bigger class — maybe fifteen girls, including Smita, Sarah, and Alexis. Alexis sat on one side of the room, but Smita, Sarah, and I sat together as our teachers, Eric and Kathryn, described what we'd be doing that semester.

Global studies is what's known at Riverbend as an "interdisciplinary period," or I.P. Each class lasts for an hour and a half instead of forty-five minutes. And each class combines subjects that are not normally taught together, in order to bring a fuller perspective to a larger topic. Understand? Not yet? I know, it's confusing at first. But it's really very simple. Basically, global studies will combine science, social studies, and English. We'll study ecological systems, anthropology of other cultures, world literature, and current events.

Sounds like a lot, doesn't it? That's why we have two teachers and plenty of time.

"I'm starving!" said Sarah as soon as class was over. "Ready for lunch?" She hooked arms with me on one side and with Smita on the other. "Meetinghouse, ho!" she cried.

I glanced back at Alexis, wondering if she was planning to join us. She was talking to Kathryn. I figured that if she'd wanted to eat lunch with me she would have mentioned it that morning when she checked out my schedule.

Lunch was fun. The dining hall was nowhere near as noisy as the SMS cafeteria, probably in part because there were no boys around. That meant nobody to start a wave of applause if you happened to trip and drop your tray, nobody to start food fights with the spaghetti and meatballs, nobody to blow straw wrappers at your head.

It was civilized, in other words.

When I thought about it, I realized that I didn't really miss boys. Sure, it felt different to be in classes with girls only, but not different *bad*. Just different. And there were even some good things about it. For example, back at SMS there were some teachers who weren't great at encouraging girls to talk in class. I'd had some problems with one teacher, Mr. Cobb, who was like that. No matter how long I held up my hand, he never called on me. But if boys yelled out the answer without even raising their hands, he listened to what they had to say. (He did apologize when I finally found the courage to point this out to him, and he made an effort to do better.) Plus, there's this attitude that girls aren't supposed to act smart, because boys might not like them.

Phooey to that.

Anyway, I hadn't had any trouble speaking out in my classes so far. Even though I was "the new girl," I felt comfortable and relaxed, and every single one of my teachers had been encouraging.

Over sandwiches and salad from the terrific salad bar, Smita, Sarah, and I discussed our morning's classes.

"J'adore Mademoiselle Orr!" Sarah declaimed, waving a breadstick dramatically. "This semester the advanced class is going to be reading French poetry. Is that cool, or what?"

She'd had French first period. Like the rest of us, she was under Kerry's spell.

"I think Kathryn's an excellent teacher too,"

Smita told us. "Plus, she and Eric have traveled to so many of the places we'll study. That's going to add a lot to the class."

For a second, I thought back to the SMS cafeteria. If I were having lunch there, I'd be sitting at a table with Jessi and a bunch of other girls. The conversation would probably be about what had been on TV last night, what weird outfit someone was wearing, boys, and whether the basketball team would win that night's game. Nobody ever talked much about classes, and if they did it was usually to complain about too much homework or a boring teacher.

Once again, I reminded myself that I had probably made the right choice.

My afternoon classes were just as good as the morning ones, with the exception of gym. Yes, gym. I hated it at SMS, and I hate it at Riverbend, even though they call it physical recreation and even though they stress noncompetitive activities such as dance and yoga. Gym is gym, that's what I say.

I felt a little lost at first in English, since it's a two-semester class and everyone else already knew one another. But I think it will be a terrific class once I feel less shy. It's called The Short Story, and all we're going to do is read short stories and discuss them. I love to read, and I love to talk about what I'm reading. The teacher's name is John. He's a little stern, but he seems genuinely interested in what his students have to say.

Even computer lab was okay. I've never been great with computers, so I was nervous. But Hannah, the teacher, made it a priority to show the new students how to set up our own e-mail accounts and learn how to sign on and write letters. I wrote a quick note to Jessi, telling her how much I liked Riverbend so far, and I begged for news from home.

My favorite afternoon class was definitely the elective I'd signed up for. As soon as I'd heard about it I knew there was no way I was going to miss out. "Creative Writing for the Stage" is its name. Yesss!

"Has anyone here ever written a play?" asked Sandy, the teacher, once we were assembled.

I raised my hand and waved it around happily. So did four of the other seven girls in the class.

"Does rewriting dialogue count?" Sarah asked with a grin. She was sitting next to me. "As an actress, that's what I usually do."

Sandy laughed. "I don't think many playwrights would be happy to hear that," she said. "But it's true that plays are not always performed exactly as written. That's part of what makes them so wonderful; the different shadings that arise when something that's written on a page comes to life in the theater."

We were off and running. Sandy led us through a great discussion, which ended with a decision that our class project would be to write and produce a series of one-act plays to be staged during a parents' weekend near the end of the semester.

I was flying high as I left the class and walked with Sarah back to Earhart. I wanted to write everything down in my journal before dinner, so I was glad to find that I had my room to myself. Alexis had told me that she often went running after classes were over.

I sat on my bed and wrote and wrote, filling page after page with descriptions of my teachers, my classes, and my new friends. I wrote down *everything*, even some doubts and fears I had about keeping up good grades at such a challenging school. I was happy at Riverbend so far, but would Riverbend be happy with me? Just as I was finishing, there was a knock at the door. It was Smita. "Come on down to the living room," she said. "We're hanging out until dinnertime."

Downstairs, I sprawled on the thick carpet of the living room with Sarah and Smita as we talked about our day. Then, suddenly, I had the strangest feeling. I checked my watch. Sure enough, it was five-thirty. Back in Stoneybrook,

Kristy was calling the BSC meeting to order. But I wasn't there. Instead of lying next to Jessi on the floor of Claudia's room, I was lying next to Smita and Sarah, here at Riverbend. It made me feel strange, and a little sad.

"Hey, Mallory, are you okay?"

Sarah must have noticed. I gave her a grateful look. "Just a little homesick, I guess."

She smiled. "I know how that can be," she said, giving me a hug.

Soon we headed for dinner. Afterward Sarah gave Smita and me a tour of the library. We stayed so long that we had to run back to Earhart to make it there by curfew, which is nine on weekdays.

I dashed up the stairs and, a little breathless, burst into my room. This time, Alexis was there. In fact, she was sitting on my bed.

Reading my journal.

CHAPTER 9

To: Mallory
From: KristyT
Subject: Aaargh!

Jessi says you wanted an update. Well, here it is. I bet you miss your brothers and sisters, but maybe this will help you appreciate the fact that you're miles away. Your siblings are out of control! Stacey and I sat for them yesterday (Monday) and they nearly drove us insane.

Kristy's e-mail was a long one. I was laughing out loud as I read it during computer lab.

She and Stacey had arrived early for an evening job at my house. My parents were going to a PTO meeting, and all the kids were home.

"You may have to do a little refereeing tonight," my dad warned Kristy and Stacey. He looked tired.

"The room issue is on everybody's minds," my mom explained, shaking her head. "We've told them that Mal's only been gone for a couple of days and we don't want to rush into any decisions, but that doesn't stop them from arguing about it."

"Endlessly," my dad added wearily. He led my mom out the door.

Kristy and Stacey looked at each other.

"Uh-oh," Stacey said.

"We can handle it," Kristy assured her.

Just then, they heard a loud banging noise coming from upstairs.

And some shrieking.

And a crash.

"Here we go!" Kristy dashed up the stairs with Stacey right behind her.

The crashes had come from Vanessa's and my room. The banging was from the room the triplets share with Nicky. The shrieking came from Margo and Claire's room.

"I'll check on the girls," Kristy told Stacey. "See what's up with the boys."

Stacey ran into the boys' room, ready for anything. She wasn't sure whether she'd be needing her first-aid training, her refereeing skills, or just good old BSC common sense.

The answer?

None of the above.

What she needed was handyman experience — at least according to Adam.

"How do you undo these bolts?" he asked Stacey as soon as she walked into the room. He sat on the floor next to one of the bunk beds, clearly frustrated. He was holding a hammer in one hand and a screwdriver in the other.

"Not by banging on them," Stacey answered. "I know that much. You'd need a wrench or something." She squatted down next to him. "By the way, hello, Adam."

"Hi, Stacey."

"Hi, Stacey," Jordan and Byron chimed in.

"Hi," Nicky called from the other side of the room. He was lying on the bottom bunk of the other set of beds.

"Want to fill me in on what's going on here?" Stacey asked.

"We're trying to take apart the beds," Jordan explained.

"I can see that. But why?"

"Because we want to move out of this

room," Adam told her. "The three of us, that is."

Stacey turned to look at Nicky. He seemed very unhappy. "Wait a minute." She frowned. "Where are you moving *to*? And why can't Nicky come?"

"We're moving into Mal's room," Adam told her, as if it were obvious. "And Nicky can't come because we're tired of living with him."

"Adam!" cried Stacey. "That's no way to talk about your brother."

"But it's true!" Jordan insisted. "He's a pest. How would you like to share your room with an eight-year-old?" He said those last words as if they were poison.

Stacey heard a sniff from the other side of the room. "What about Nicky?" she asked.

"I'm not moving anywhere," Nicky said, wiping his eyes. His voice was surprisingly steady. "And neither is this bed."

"What do you mean?" Stacey asked.

"He chained himself to the bed," said Adam in a disgusted voice. "With a bicycle lock. And he chained the bed to the bookshelf."

Stacey smiled to herself. So Nicky wasn't going to let this happen without a fight. Good for him. "What about you, Byron? What do you think about all this?" Byron was sitting on the floor near the bookcase, leafing through a comic book.

He shrugged. "I don't know," he muttered. "I guess it doesn't matter much to me."

"Come on, bro!" Jordan exclaimed. "All for one and one for all, remember?"

"Whatever." Byron sighed and returned to his comic.

"So will you help us?" Adam asked Stacey, gesturing toward the bolts on the bed.

Stacey shook her head. "Nope. First of all, I don't like the way you're treating Nicky. Second, I have no idea how to take the bed apart. And finally, nothing has been decided yet. So you guys are just going to have to cool your jets."

Adam and Jordan groaned.

Just then, Kristy poked her head in the room. "Everything okay in here?" she asked.

Stacey nodded. "Just fine." She left the boys' room to join Kristy in the hall. "Except that we're going to have to unlock Nicky. What's up with Claire and Margo?"

"Unlock Nicky?" Kristy repeated, bewildered.

"I'll explain later."

"Okay. Meanwhile, the screaming was Claire, throwing one of her tantrums."

"I bet I can guess what it was about," Stacey said.

Kristy nodded. "Margo's upset too. She keeps saying 'Why not me? Why can't *I* have my own room?' It's that middle-child thing. She feels overlooked."

"What about the crash from Vanessa's room?" Stacey asked.

"I'm on my way there now," Kristy admitted. "It took awhile to convince Claire not to hold her breath until she turned blue."

Stacey and Kristy headed down the hall and knocked on Vanessa's door.

"Just a sec!" she called out.

They heard more crashes and the scraping sound of furniture being moved.

Then Vanessa opened the door a crack. She was flushed, and there was a smear of dust on her nose. "Hi!" she said brightly without opening the door any farther.

"What's going on in there, Vanessa?" Kristy asked.

"Nothing." Vanessa's flush deepened. "Why do you ask?"

"We've been hearing some strange noises," said Stacey.

"Oh, that."

"Yes, that," Kristy said.

"I'm just — rearranging things a little."

"Really? Let's see." Kristy wasn't going to let her off the hook.

Grudgingly, Vanessa let them in.

Stacey and Kristy took one quick look around and understood what was going on.

Vanessa was claiming the whole room for herself, no question about it. She'd moved the two beds together to make one big one, put my bookcase next to her own, and dragged her bureau to where my bed used to be.

"Nice," said Kristy.

Vanessa beamed.

"Too bad you'll have to move it all back again."

Vanessa's face fell.

"You can't just claim this room for yourself," Stacey told her gently. "It's something that has to be worked out with the whole family."

"But I need peace and quiet for writing poetry," Vanessa wailed. "I deserve this room." She ran to her desk and grabbed a piece of cardboard. "See? I already made a sign." She showed it to Kristy and Stacey.

Poet at work
Knock, you silly jerk.

"Lovely," murmured Kristy. Then her voice grew stern. "Look, we're not going to work this out today. Your parents don't want to rush into a decision. So why don't we all go downstairs and do something fun together?"

Good idea, thought Stacey. Distract the kids and give them something else to think about.

Unfortunately, that didn't work. No matter what activities Kristy and Stacey came up with, my brothers and sisters managed to bring the subject back to the Room Wars again.

A Monopoly game ended in a fight when Adam offered to give Park Place to Vanessa — in exchange for rights to the room.

When Kristy and Stacey opened their Kid-Kits and passed out markers, all the kids ended up making signs for their own rooms.

Stacey suggested writing letters to me. Guess what the letters were about?

Kristy suggested baking cookies. Margo and Claire tried to bribe Vanessa with extra chocolate chips.

Finally, Kristy and Stacey gave up and ordered everyone to work on homework for the rest of the evening. But by that time, nobody could concentrate. The Room Wars were the only thing on anyone's mind.

"So you see," Kristy's e-mail ended, "you should consider yourself lucky to be out of this house!"

You know what, though? It's funny. I'd been doing pretty well at fighting off any homesickness — until then. This may sound crazy, but suddenly I missed my siblings more than ever.

CHAPTER 10

"Your *journal*? How dare she?" Smita stared at me, openmouthed. The muffin she'd been eating lay forgotten on her plate.

Tuesday morning. Breakfast. I was telling Sarah and Smita what had happened the night before. It was only my second day of classes at Riverbend. How could it be that things were already such a mess with Alexis?

"She tried to hide it when I first came in," I said. "She shoved it under the pillow. So she knew what she was doing wasn't right."

"You bet she did," Sarah said grimly. "So what did you do?"

"I confronted her," I said.

"And?" Smita asked.

"She admitted it. And she handed it over." I ate a spoonful of my blueberry yogurt, even though I didn't have much of an appetite. In fact, my stomach was in a knot. As far as I knew, nobody had ever read my journal. I'd never even thought about censoring what I wrote in my book; it is the one place where I am always totally honest. I pour myself into what I write, and knowing that Alexis had read my most private thoughts made me feel sick to my stomach.

"She said I had left it open on my bed," I told Sarah and Smita. "She said it was practically an invitation to read it."

Sarah rolled her eyes. "Oh, please. Even if you *did* leave your journal open, you obviously didn't mean for anyone to read it."

"That's right," Smita agreed. "A real friend would ask first."

"Anyway, I didn't leave it open," I said. "At least, I'm pretty sure I didn't. I can't be positive." Alexis had a way of making me question my own memory.

"Either way, it doesn't matter," Sarah told me. "Smita's right. If one of us saw your journal lying open, we wouldn't read it without asking."

I smiled at her. Smita had said that's what a "real friend" would do. Sarah was telling me that she and Smita fell into that category. That felt nice. As long as I had them, maybe I could just ignore the Alexis problem. If I didn't pay attention to it, maybe it would disappear.

But the problem was living in my room.

"You know what the worst part is?" I said.

"She told me that it wasn't as if I'd written anything interesting anyway. That really bugged me."

"Like she's some literary critic." Sarah snorted. She shook her head, tossing her curls. "That girl is way out of line."

I told Sarah and Smita more about Alexis. Things hadn't improved after the journal episode. Instead, they'd gone downhill. For the rest of the evening she'd been extra bossy, lecturing me about the way I'd left my bed mussed (not unmade — just mussed) that morning and informing me that I'd have to do something about the overcrowding in my drawers. (Huh?) She badmouthed Smita and Sarah (I didn't tell them that part), "explaining" to me that it wasn't wise to make friends without checking them out first.

She even accused me of using some of her toothpaste.

"Whoa," Smita murmured, when I reported that.

"I believe it!" cried Sarah. "I'd believe anything you told me about her. Know why? Because I've heard it all before." She folded her arms and raised her eyebrows, looking mysterious.

"What?" I asked. "What do you mean?"

"I wasn't going to tell you," she said. "I thought you'd want to give Alexis a chance.

But the way she's acting? It's nothing new. She's already been through two roommates this year."

"You're kidding," Smita said.

"I am absolutely not kidding. I wish I were."

"So, tell all," I said, leaning forward. "Who were the other roommates? What happened?"

Smita looked interested too. "Normally I hate gossip," she said solemnly. "But this is important. If Mal is going to work things out with Alexis, she needs information."

"Well, I love gossip," said Sarah. "But you're right. This isn't about dishing dirt on Alexis. It's just about understanding the situation. So here goes." She took a deep breath.

"The first roommate was Amy Burdick. That's who Alexis started out the year with. And from what I've heard, Alexis treated Amy about the same way she's treating you. Maybe worse."

"What happened to Amy?" I asked. "I don't think I've met her."

"You haven't," Sarah said grimly. "She left school."

I gasped. So did Smita. Sarah looked like she was enjoying the drama of the moment.

"You mean Alexis drove her out of Riverbend?" I asked, horrified.

"Well, not exactly," Sarah admitted. "I think there were a lot of reasons Amy left. She was having a hard time in her classes, and then her grandmother died in the middle of the semester. But I have to believe that Alexis's attitude didn't make things any easier for her." Sarah paused to take a bite of her bagel.

I shoved my yogurt aside. My appetite was gone.

Smita checked her watch. "It's almost time for class," she said. "What about the other girl?"

"She's still here," Sarah told us. "She spent the second half of last semester as Alexis's roomie, but just before break she switched to a single room. Her name's Jen Bodner, and she lives on the third floor in Earhart."

"I think I've met her," said Smita. "She seems nice."

"She is," Sarah agreed. "But I can tell you that she has nothing to do with Alexis. They don't even speak when they pass each other on campus."

"Sounds like I need to meet this person," I said. "Will you introduce me?"

"Gladly. I bet you two will have plenty to talk about."

I had a feeling she was right. I already felt better, in a way, knowing that I wasn't the first roomie Alexis had been hard on. It's like that old saying: "Misery loves company."

Until I had a chance to meet Jen, I decided

that the best policy was to forget Alexis and concentrate on everything good about River- bend. Terrific classes, excellent teachers, great new friends . . . there was plenty to be happy about.

But forgetting Alexis was not so easy.

After all, Riverbend is not a big school. And on Tuesday, I found out exactly how small it is. Small enough to make it very, very hard to avoid someone you'd rather not see.

I bumped into her right away, on my way to math class. Smita was with me, but Alexis ig- nored her. "Hi, Mal!" she said with a big smile.

As if nothing had happened.

"You ran out so early this morning I didn't even have the chance to ask," Alexis went on, "but I knew you wouldn't mind."

"Mind what?" I asked.

"Mind my borrowing these," she said, turn- ing her head to show me the earrings she was wearing.

Horseshoe earrings. My favorites. Given to me by Jessi.

"Alexis —" I began, exasperated.

"Great!" she said. "I knew you'd be cool about it. See you!" She took off down the walk, leaving me and Smita to fume.

Later, in global studies, she humiliated me by quoting something I'd written in my journal about how good-looking our teacher Eric is.

True, she whispered it in my ear so nobody else heard, but still. I was so embarrassed and so mad I could hardly see straight.

Then, at lunch, she somehow managed to make me feel sorry for her. Ridiculous, right? I can't help it. There I was, sitting with my new friends. We were talking a mile a minute — *not* about Alexis, by the way — and laughing and having a grand old time. Alexis? She was sitting by herself, looking awfully lonely. Something in her face made me sad. I had to fight the urge to invite her to sit at our table.

Finally, in our short-story class, when John asked if anyone had any comments about the discussion we'd had the day before, Alexis raised her hand. "I was thinking about what you said about how short stories are like little worlds," she said. "I think that's what I love about them. It's like the best writers give you the chance to step into another life for a little while and experience it fully."

"Excellent comment," said John.

Alexis tried to look modest. "Thanks," she said. I stared at her, hard. She avoided my eyes.

That comment was something I'd written in my journal.

I couldn't believe it. But what could I do? It wasn't worth making a scene over.

I went overboard trying to avoid Alexis for the rest of the day, and I succeeded. Until I had to go to bed, when I had no choice but to head for my room.

Alexis was already in bed when I let myself in. She sat up and turned on a light. "Mallory?" she asked in a little voice. "I'm sorry. Really. Sometimes I don't know why I do the things I do. I know I upset you."

I didn't know what to say. "That's okay," I mumbled. She sounded truly apologetic.

"I didn't even *look* for your journal today," she said with a little grin.

"Doesn't matter," I replied. "You wouldn't have found it." I'd hidden it really well, in a secret pocket of the suitcase I'd stashed under my bed.

"And I put the earrings back," she continued.

"Good," I said. She was making an effort to apologize, but I wasn't sure how long it would last. I went down the hall to brush my teeth.

When I came back, Alexis was her old self again. While talking to me again about the closet situation, she somehow managed to mention that Sarah couldn't always be trusted, and she told me that Smita seemed "sweet but boring."

I tried to tune her out, but she was on a roll. Finally, I told her I had to sleep. I turned off my light and rolled over. I didn't know what else to do. After all, I'd never shared a room with anybody but Vanessa, and we'd always been able to work out our differences.

Alexis turned her light out soon after I'd pretended to go to sleep. I lay there in the dark, wide-awake. Eventually, I dozed off, but I never fell into a deep sleep. Instead, I tossed and turned all night.

And every time I woke up, I saw Alexis's form in the bed across the room.

CHAPTER 11

The next morning, I left the room before Alexis woke up. And then I did everything I could to avoid her. It seemed easier to stay away.

Still, it wasn't actually simple. Avoiding Alexis meant dodging her between classes, making sure to sit as far away as possible from her at mealtimes, and staying away from my room except for the time I spent sleeping there.

That meant I had to do all my studying in the library, the living room, or friends' rooms. It meant I had no time just to be alone, to write in my journal in peace, or to lie on my bed and read a book for pleasure.

Smita and Sarah were great. I was welcome in their rooms anytime, and they helped me keep tabs on Alexis's whereabouts. Sarah, especially, loved the intrigue of mapping out Alexis's movements. "She's heading for the library," she'd hiss to me as we left the meetinghouse after dinner. "That means you can stop by your room to pick up your notebook. We'll meet you in my room in fifteen minutes." I was surprised she didn't suggest we synchronize our watches.

Meanwhile, if you didn't count the Alexis problem, I was having an incredibly great time at Riverbend. I felt I'd finally found a place where I belonged. I loved my classes, my teachers, and my new friends. And I was so busy that I hardly had time to be homesick.

I mean, of course I missed my family and my friends in the BSC — but not so much that I was miserable being away from them. In fact, I wondered if this was how Jessi felt when she'd gone to a special ballet program in New York not long ago. I missed her terribly, but I bet she was too busy and happy to think much about her friends at home.

However, there *was* the Alexis problem. Even though I tried to avoid her, we managed to bump into each other several times every day. And just about every time, she said or did something that annoyed me, embarrassed me, or made me feel bad. Occasionally she'd act pleasant, but I'd already learned not to trust her. It never lasted.

"I know exactly what you mean," Jen Bodner told me. Sarah introduced us Wednesday night after dinner and left us alone to talk. "It never lasted for me either."

Jen was great. She was easy to talk to and we had something in common anyway.

"She drove me up a wall," Jen reported. "I mean, I wanted to be friends with her. I tried my hardest. Here I am, a nice, friendly Jewish girl from Boston. What's not to like? But Alexis didn't give me a chance. She didn't want another roommate. When Amy left, I think she assumed she'd be able to have the room to herself. So she made me feel like a trespasser from the beginning."

I was nodding. "That's how I feel. Like it's her world, and I'm just in the way. She didn't even move her stuff so I could have room for my things."

Jen laughed. "Sounds familiar. And are there lots of rules?"

"Yes!" I cried, laughing as well. "Oh, the rules go on forever. Study hour from four to six. Take —"

"Take your shoes off when you come in the room!" Jen interrupted. "Oh, sure. I know them all. It's like she's queen or something. I mean, room rules are fine if both roomies agree on them. But Alexis doesn't even ask. She just tells you what she expects."

"I don't think she's a bad person," I said. "She's just hard to get along with."

Jen agreed. "Very hard. Life is a lot easier now that I have a room of my own." She waved a hand around her room. It was smaller than the room I shared with Alexis, with room for only one bed. Still, Jen had plenty of space and plenty of privacy. But I wasn't sure I'd want to live alone, the way she did. I'm used to sharing a room with someone, and for me, part of the boarding school experience was having a roommate. I knew I might feel lonely if I were on my own. But I didn't say anything about that to Jen.

"You should talk to Pam," Jen suggested. "She might be able to help you work things out. I mean, she's been at Riverbend since she was in fifth grade. She's seen it all."

"I don't know," I said hesitantly. "I don't want to be seen as a complainer. I feel better just talking to you. Now I know I'm not crazy to think Alexis is difficult to live with."

"But talking to me isn't going to change anything," Jen pointed out. "I'm glad to discuss it, but you're still going to have to at least *sleep* in your room every night. Alexis isn't going to disappear."

"I know," I said, sighing. "I know."

"So talk to Pam. I'll even come with you if you want."

"I'll think about it," I promised.

And I did. I thought about it a lot over the next couple of days. But I still wasn't ready to talk to Pam. Telling her about the trouble with

Alexis would make it official. I'd wait until I was sure I couldn't work things out on my own.

Meanwhile, I threw myself into my classes. I liked them all — with the possible exception of gym. Math class was hard but still enjoyable; Amy said I had a "hidden talent" for numbers, something I'd never heard from any math teacher before. In French, we'd begun to have short conversations about the weather. I was struggling a bit with my vocabulary and tenses, but Kerry told me (after class, in English) I had an excellent accent. In global studies we were studying the ecology of the rain forest, and we'd broken up into small groups to work on projects that combined art, science, and language. (Fortunately, Alexis was not in my small group.) My short-story class was reading O. Henry, and John had led us into some amazing discussions.

But my favorite class, hands down, was Creative Writing for the Stage. Sarah and I were already working hard on a midterm project, a scene that I would write and she would star in. We were so excited about it that we drove everybody else nuts. We couldn't stop talking about it. Even patient Smita finally told us to be quiet, after we'd babbled all the way through Thursday night's dinner.

I stayed out of my room until bedtime on

Thursday, then slipped in quietly, hoping Alexis would already be asleep.

She wasn't.

"Hello, stranger," she said as I came in. She was lying in bed, reading.

"Hi," I answered a little nervously. I sat down on my bed. I wanted to check for my journal, to make sure she hadn't somehow found it and read it again. But if I checked for it, she'd see me and I'd have to find another hiding place. I'd have to wait until our lights were out before I went rummaging around. Which meant it would be too dark to write anything. I hadn't filled many pages in the last few days, that was for sure.

"Did you have a good day?" Alexis seemed to want to talk.

I nodded. "Sure, it was great," I said. I yawned. "I'm tired, though. I think I'm going to hit the sack."

"Right." Alexis's voice was flat. "I think I get the picture. You have your friends. You don't need to talk to me."

"But —" She was the one who'd been un-friendly.

"That's fine," she said, reaching up to snap off her light. "Sleep well, Mallory."

I didn't, of course. She'd made me feel terrible. Was it mean to avoid her? She seemed hurt. I hadn't meant to make her feel that way.

101

I've always prided myself on being a good friend — and I'd have liked to be a friend to her. But she'd been so prickly and so hard to deal with. I didn't think it was *my* fault we weren't getting along.

The next morning, I woke up feeling bleary. Alexis was already dressed and on her way out the door. "I won't be around this evening," she said. "I'm going on the Friday night movie trip into town. So you can have the room to yourself."

I wondered what the Friday night movie trip was, but a night on my own sounded very, very good. I tried not to let my face show how glad I was to hear the news. "Have fun," I said.

"Sure," she said. " 'Bye." She was out the door. And I hardly saw her for the rest of the day. The funny thing? I was kind of sorry. I had a lingering feeling, like a bad taste in my mouth.

That night, after dinner, I sat on my bed and wrote in my journal for over an hour. It felt great to catch up. Just as I was finishing, there was a knock at the door and Pam stuck her head in.

"Hi," I said, surprised.

"Hi, Mallory. Just checking in to see how things are going. You've been here for almost a week now."

Only a week? It seemed like months. "Everything's great," I said enthusiastically. "I love my classes. Have you ever taken global studies with Eric and Kathryn? They're excellent. And I'm having a great time with Sarah and Smita. And the food is great." I was babbling; I knew it. And I was talking about everything except the roommate problem. It was a subject I wanted to avoid.

"And you're all settled in here?" Pam asked, waving a hand around the room.

"Oh, sure," I said. "It's very comfortable."

Pam nodded.

"But — " I began. I was thinking of what Jen had said when she urged me to talk to Pam. About how she might be able to help me work things out. Maybe it wasn't such a bad idea. After all, I hadn't been able to figure anything out on my own.

Suddenly, I felt the whole story spilling out of me. I told Pam everything about Alexis: the rules, the bossiness, the way she'd claimed the room. And I told her how I'd tried avoiding Alexis, and how she'd made me feel bad about that. I tried to make it clear that I loved everything else about Riverbend, but that I just couldn't stand being in the room when Alexis was around.

Pam just listened and nodded. Finally, when I'd wound down, she gave me a little hug. "I know it's hard, Mallory," she said. "I understand that Alexis isn't easy to live with. Can I just ask — have you tried talking this out with her?"

I gaped at Pam. "Talking it out? With Alexis?"

She nodded. "It might be worth a try. Maybe things would improve if you could just clear the air a bit. Start over."

I was doubtful. "I don't know," I said.

"Would you give it a try?" Pam asked gently.

"Sure," I said, shrugging. "I guess I have nothing to lose. I'll try."

"That's the spirit. I'll check back with you to see how it went. Good luck!" She stood up and gave me one last pat on the shoulder. Then she left.

I spent the next hour trying desperately to think of what on earth I was going to say to Alexis when she came home from the movies.

CHAPTER 12

By the time Alexis walked into the room, I was a nervous wreck. I knew we had to try to work things out, but I still had no idea how we were going to do it. I should be better at talking things over. After all, in a big family you learn to deal with interpersonal problems before they get out of hand. And Jessi and I have been through our share of difficult times: misunderstandings, hurt feelings, things like that.

But this was different.

With both my family and Jessi there was a foundation of love and friendship. I didn't have anything like that with Alexis. Also, Alexis was — well, Alexis. One thing I could count on was that she wasn't going to make it easy for me.

When the door swung open and she strolled into the room, it was all I could do to smile and try to act normal. "Hi! How was the movie?"

Alexis shrugged. "Okay, I guess." She didn't

105

look at me. Instead, she concentrated on taking off her shoes.

"I heard it isn't as scary as the first one," I said.

"I wouldn't know. I never saw the other one." She shrugged out of her jacket and hung it up.

"I didn't either," I confessed. "I don't really like scary movies."

She didn't answer.

"I like romantic movies or stories about animals," I went on. "You know, like *The Black Stallion*. That's one of my favorites. That and *The Incredible Journey*. Did you ever see that?"

Alexis looked at me. "You sure are chatty tonight," she said. "You've barely said three words to me all week, and now you want to discuss the cinema in detail?"

I blushed. Then I took a deep breath. "Actually, no," I said. "But there is something else I'd like to discuss."

"What is it?"

I took another deep breath. "It's just — it's just that I feel like we're not getting along so well. And I was wondering if we could try to start over."

Alexis was silent for a moment. She was sitting on her bed, and she'd picked up a nail file. She went to work on her thumbnail while I waited anxiously to see what she'd say next. "Apology accepted," she said finally.

My mouth fell open. "What?"

"I figure you're trying to say you're sorry for the way you've been acting," said Alexis calmly. "I mean, you've been treating me like I have bubonic plague or something. You avoid me during the day and only come in here to sleep. Well, I have to admit that it has hurt my feelings a little. But I can probably put it behind me."

I was flabbergasted. (Don't you love that word?)

And speechless.

For a moment. Then I managed to squeak something out. "That's — that's not exactly what I meant," I said. Clearly, I was going to have to be a little more straightforward with Alexis.

"Oh?" She arched an eyebrow. "So what *did* you mean?"

She really *wasn't* going to make this easy for me. "Well," I began, trying to collect my thoughts, "I guess part of the reason I've been avoiding the room is because I don't exactly feel welcome here."

"Not welcome? In what way?"

I felt like asking if she had a few hours for me to list all the ways. Instead, I mumbled something about her not leaving me any space on the dresser or in the closet.

"You're kidding," she said. "So that's the problem? Why didn't you just say something?" She stood up and walked to the dresser. Then she ran her arm across the top, pushing all her stuff over to one side. "There. Done. Help yourself." She plopped back down on the bed.

"Alexis, I —" Clearly, I was making her mad. But I was mad too. She was twisting everything I said. "Look," I continued, "it's not just the dresser. It's the rules too — the rules that you made up without consulting me. And the fact that you read my journal. And borrowed my earrings without asking."

"I apologized for those things," Alexis replied. "Why do you have to keep bringing them up? It's like you *want* to be mad at me. And anyway, if you want to be such close pals, then we should be able to share things like journals and earrings." Now she looked hurt.

"I don't share my journal with anyone," I said stiffly. "And those earrings happen to have a lot of sentimental value to me."

"Whatever," said Alexis, yawning. "I won't take them again. And I won't read your boring journal. I already told you that."

I felt my face growing hot. "Look, it's not about the journal or the earrings," I said, trying hard not to let my voice shake. "It's about fairness. And sharing the room as equals. Something you don't seem to be very good at, as I'm sure Amy and Jen would agree."

Her head snapped up. "Amy and Jen?" she asked. "Oh, so you've heard some gossip and now you think you know it all. Well, you're wrong. There are two sides to every story, you know."

"Sure," I snapped. "There's your side, and then there's your side." I couldn't believe I had said that. But I was tired of arguing with Alexis. This wasn't how our talk was supposed to go. In fact, if it went on any longer, I had the feeling both of us might say things we would regret. We might never be able to repair the damage. "Look," I said in a softer voice, "let's drop this for now. We're not making any progress anyway. Maybe we can talk about it tomorrow, when we're not so tired."

"Fine," Alexis spat. By then she was lying on her bed. She turned over so her back was facing me.

I grabbed my toothbrush and marched down the hall to the bathroom. Once there, I squeezed toothpaste out of the tube and started brushing so hard I practically felt my gums screaming.

"Hey, girl, take it easy!" That was Sarah, who

had come in behind me. She was giving me an amused look in the mirror. "What's the matter?"

I was so glad to see her I nearly started crying. I spat out my toothpaste, rinsed, and told her the whole ugly story.

She was sympathetic and full of indignation. "That girl needs to go back to kindergarten and learn how to be a civilized person," she declared. "What is her problem?"

"I don't know. I knew it wasn't going to be easy to talk things out, but I didn't think it would go *that* badly."

"She's just —" Sarah began. But Alexis walked in then and Sarah stopped in midsentence. I'm sure Alexis noticed, but she didn't say a word. She just walked to the sink that was farthest away, brushed her teeth, and left.

When I came back into the room, she was already under the covers, asleep — or pretending to be. We didn't talk anymore that night.

I woke up early, but Alexis must have been up even earlier. Her bed was empty. Where had she gone?

Then I remembered. It was Saturday. The day Riverbend students do community service. I'd be out on my first assignment today. And Alexis must have already left for hers. I decided to put my troubles out of my mind and enjoy the day.

Sarah blew into my room a few minutes

later. "How are you feeling today?" she asked. "Ready to take on a bunch of wild kids?"

"You bet," I answered. "In fact, I can't wait."

Sarah was in my community-service group. So were Jen and Pam. I knew we were going to have a terrific time. This week we'd be helping out at the Easton Public Library, where the children's room sponsored a weekly Saturday morning movie festival for kids. Parents were invited to drop off their children, and many of them took advantage of the offer. The children's library didn't have enough staff to supervise so many kids, so we Riverbend students were going to help out. The job was right up my alley.

After breakfast, six of us piled into a minivan. Our French teacher, Kerry, drove us into Easton. For my benefit, she played the part of tour guide as we drove along. She pointed out the lake where we'd be able to swim in spring, a favorite snack bar, a mountain that was traditional to climb on Easter morning. We drove past Edgewood, a boys' boarding school, and Kerry told me that I'd have a chance to meet Edgewood students at Riverbend's annual May Day dance, if not sooner. Sarah elbowed me at that point and mouthed something about "stuck-up snobs." Pam noticed and laughed. "True," she admitted, "but some of them are cute too."

That sent everyone else in the van into reminiscing about past May Day dances and romances with boys from Edgewood. The ride to Easton went quickly, and soon we were pulling up in front of the library.

The children's room was bright and welcoming. And *full* of excited, happy kids. The films weren't due to start for half an hour, but the place had already filled up and the kids needed attention. I felt at home right away. Spotting a little girl who looked on the verge of either tears or a tantrum, I introduced myself and took her to a quiet corner where I could read to her. Soon she was snuggled next to me, listening contentedly to the story of Curious George's trip to the zoo.

At that moment, the problems with Alexis seemed very, very far away.

I returned a little later, when the kids were mostly settled in. Pam pulled me aside to ask how things had gone. "Were you and Alexis able to work things out?" she asked.

I shook my head. "We didn't even come close," I said. Then I told her what had happened.

Pam frowned. "I'm sorry, Mallory," she said. "I know Alexis is hard to deal with, but try to understand that she's dealing with some issues of her own. I don't think she's very happy, and it might be hard for her to watch how easily you've fit in at Riverbend." She stopped herself. Maybe she'd realized that she shouldn't talk to me about Alexis's feelings. "But no matter what, the problem between the two of you still needs to be resolved. Maybe I need to sit down with both of you and see if we can talk this through."

I wasn't thrilled with the idea of facing Alexis again, but maybe with Pam's help we'd do a little better. "I'm willing to try," I said. "I'm not so sure about Alexis, though."

Just then, a boy of about ten came running over to us. "I think I have to throw up!" he announced.

I swung into action, grabbing him and pulling him toward the bathroom. "You can make it," I said. "See you, Pam!" I called over my shoulder.

We made it.

The rest of the morning flew by. After the movies we helped serve a snack and then spent an hour or so playing organized games and reading out loud. It was majorly fun. In fact, I had such a great time with the kids and with the other Riverbend students that I almost forgot about Alexis.

Almost.

CHAPTER 13

To: Mallory
From: AbbyS
Subject: Peace at last!

BULLETIN: A settlement has finally been reached in the Pike Room Wars.

—It wasnt easy, eether. (Thats me, Claud. On Abby's email.)

Ambassador Stevenson and Ambassador Kishi will be awarded the Silver Doorknob for helping to work out the situation.

—What am I gong to do with a sliver doorknob?

You'll probably make an earring out of it. Anyway, Mal, here's how it all came together:

Abby's e-mail went on for quite awhile. I read happily, glad to hear how things had finally calmed down back at home. (I'd had a quick phone call about it the night before — Saturday — just to see if I agreed with the solution. But I hadn't heard much about how it had come together.)

Maybe I couldn't work out my roommate problems, but at least my brothers and sisters had worked out theirs.

Anyway, as Abby explained it, the evening started with my parents practically running out the door as soon as she and Claudia arrived. "They were headed to the movies," Abby wrote. "And I don't think they were late. But they looked as if they couldn't wait to leave the house."

When they saw the state my siblings were in, Abby and Claudia agreed that they couldn't blame my parents for bolting out of there.

Nicky and Adam were in the kitchen, squabbling.

Vanessa and Margo were in the living room, quarreling.

Jordan and Claire were on the second-floor landing, having words.

Byron was sulking by himself in the rec room.

Ugh.

Abby and Claudia went to work. Abby headed to the kitchen to separate Nicky and Adam, while Claudia went upstairs to mediate between Jordan and Claire (Claire was working herself into a full-scale tantrum). Then they met in the living room to make peace between Vanessa and Margo. They gathered all the kids together there to talk.

For about three seconds, the house was quiet and peaceful.

Then the yelling started all over again.

"Tell Jordan to give up!" Vanessa shouted. "It's my room, and he can't have it." She folded her arms and stuck out her lower lip.

"Tell *her* to quit boasting about it," Adam yelled back. "Did you hear her latest poem? It goes, 'A single room is not to be had, even by the likes of Mom and Dad.' " He quoted Vanessa in a high, singsong voice. "Aaugh!" he added at the end of his recitation.

"And tell her she can't kick me out of my bed," Margo put in. "I don't mind if she visits us, but the bed's not big enough for both of us. Last night I ended up on the floor."

"What's this?" Abby asked.

"Vanessa has been hanging out in our room," said Margo. "Even though she has her own gigundo room, she has to squeeze into ours. And last night she even slept in there. In my bed."

Abby and Claudia exchanged glances. Interesting. So Vanessa was feeling lonesome in that big, old room. She seemed to like the idea of her own room better than the reality of it.

"Who cares about your stupid room!" Vanessa yelled. "I'll never come in there again, if that's what you want. I'll just stay in my room. My *single* room."

"Fine!" said Margo.

"Fine!" echoed Claire, adding a stamp of her foot for emphasis.

"Not fine!" yelled Nicky. "It's not your room for keeps. Mom and Dad said so."

"That's right," Adam said, agreeing for once with his younger brother. "So don't start acting like that room belongs to you. Or else."

"Or else what?" Vanessa asked teasingly.

Abby stuck two fingers in her mouth and whistled loudly. "Hold it right there," she shouted. Then she dropped her voice. "This is ridiculous. You guys could go on fighting about this all night."

"But you're not going to," said Claudia, jumping in to support Abby. "You're going to — um —"

"Do homework," finished Abby decisively. "I don't care if it is Saturday night," she added, holding up a hand to ward off any arguments. "I want you all to go to your own rooms and do any homework you have. If you don't have any, you can just read or color quietly. And after an hour, if nobody's started any new fights, we'll make some popcorn and watch a video together."

The kids were too shocked to argue. Abby had put her foot down, and there was no point in questioning her. Especially when Claudia was there too, arms folded like a drill sergeant's, ready to enforce Abby's orders. Meekly, they climbed the stairs and headed into their rooms.

Abby and Claudia exchanged a high five. Then they headed for the kitchen to make sure there was popcorn in the cabinets.

Little did they know that another storm was brewing.

Ten minutes later, it broke loose.

There was the sudden sound of pounding feet and slamming doors from upstairs. A chorus of shouts and cries. More pounding feet, more slamming doors.

Abby and Claudia ran up the stairs and into Vanessa's room.

"What — ?" asked Abby when she surveyed the scene. Every one of my brothers and sisters but Byron was stuffed into Vanessa's room. Vanessa looked furious.

"It's ours!" Adam yelled. He held up a drawing of a flag showing three boys against a field of purple stars. "We claim this room for ourselves."

Adam and Jordan had stormed Vanessa's room. The wars had escalated.

"No, it's mine, all mine!" Nicky shouted gleefully. He was bouncing on Vanessa's bed.

"Wrong!" sang out Margo. She twirled around in the middle of the room. "This is a girls' room, all the way. Claire and I claim it."

"We claim it, we claim it, we dirty, rotten claim it," sang Claire.

"Where's Byron?" asked Claudia, confused.

"He's down in the rec room," Jordan answered disgustedly. "He says he doesn't care."

"That's because he knows this room is mine," Vanessa said. "Mine. MINE!" She was yelling at the top of her lungs as she tried to shove Margo out the door.

A little worried, Abby left Claudia to deal with the Siege of Vanessa's Room and went downstairs to check on Byron. "What's up?" she asked him when she found him reading quietly in the rec room. "Don't you have any opinion about this room issue?"

He shook his head. "Not really," he answered. "The whole thing is dumb. Jordan and Adam are acting like babies. Which is kind of funny, since they're always telling Nicky what a baby he is. Which he isn't, really."

Abby nodded thoughtfully.

"So you're staying out of the Room Wars?" she asked.

He nodded. "However it works out is fine with me. I just want some peace and quiet."

"Don't we all," Abby said under her breath. She headed back upstairs to find the siege continuing. Claudia was trying to convince the kids to go back to their own rooms, but nobody was about to budge.

The boys insisted that they'd claimed the room.

Margo and Claire weren't about to let that happen.

And Vanessa shouted that they were all trespassing.

Finally, Claudia and Abby realized there was nothing they could do, short of physically lifting and moving each of the kids. So they held back and kept an eye on things.

My parents arrived home an hour or so later. Claudia and Abby filled them in on what was going on. Mom and Dad weren't — to put it mildly — too happy about the situation.

"Okay, enough is enough," my dad announced. "I'm calling a family conference, and we're going to work this out. Now."

My mom invited Claudia and Abby to stay. "Maybe you can help us solve this problem," she said. "If you can, we'll pay you double for your time tonight. It would be worth every penny."

Claudia and Abby said they wouldn't think of taking extra pay. But they were happy to stay, mostly out of curiosity.

Soon the Pike family (minus me, of course) was gathered in the living room. "Okay," my dad began, "I want each of you to tell me what you think should be done with the room that once belonged to Vanessa and Mal."

Everybody started yelling at once, almost before he'd finished the sentence.

He held up his hands. "Wait!" he yelled. "Wait!"

Abby whistled again. Everybody fell silent.

"Thank you," my dad told Abby. Then he turned back to my brothers and sisters. "One at a time, please," he said wearily. "Claire, why don't you go first."

Each of the kids stated their case. My parents listened carefully, nodding. Finally, everything was being laid out in an organized manner.

But it didn't help. There still didn't seem to be a solution. Three rooms, seven kids. Was there any way to be fair to everyone?

Suddenly, Abby sat up straight. She'd been gazing at Byron and thinking. "Byron," she said, "let me ask you something. Would you mind sharing a room with Nicky?"

Byron hesitated.

Jordan and Adam looked at each other. "NO WAY!" they yelled.

Byron glanced at them and frowned. Then he

took a deep breath — and shook his head. "No, I wouldn't mind," he said quietly.

Nicky's smile lit up the living room.

"Whoa!" said Claudia. "Step one. And I think I have an idea for step two. Vanessa, how would you like to live with Claire and Margo? If there was enough space for everyone, that is?"

Vanessa looked down at the floor. "Actually," she admitted in a small voice, "I think I'd like that."

"You can *definitely* live with us," said Margo, jumping up to hug Vanessa. "We only stormed your room because we didn't want the boys to get their way without a fight."

My parents took it from there. And, by bedtime, the plan was set: Vanessa, Claire, Margo — and all of my stuff — would move into the big room the boys had been living in. (That's the part they called me to check out.) Byron and Nicky would move into Margo and Claire's old room. And Jordan and Adam would share the room that used to belong to Vanessa and me.

Everyone was happy. And life in the Pike household would soon be back to normal . . . without me.

CHAPTER 14

Meanwhile, back at Riverbend, things were not going nearly as smoothly. On Monday, I once again began avoiding my room — and Alexis — as much as possible.

I had thought some more about Pam's idea of having us all sit down together, and I'd realized it was probably the only way Alexis and I would ever work things out. But there was one problem. I couldn't figure out a way to bring the idea up with Alexis.

Especially since we had hardly exchanged three words since Friday night.

After classes on Monday, I stopped by the mailroom in the administration building and found a big box, plastered with stickers, waiting for me. A care package from my BSC friends! Sarah and Smita helped me lug it back to Earhart. Alexis was out, so we brought it to my room and opened it. I felt my eyes fill with tears when I saw what my friends had sent me.

Suddenly, I missed them all very much. There was a huge box of chocolate chip cookies — homemade ones, from Claudia — and cards from everyone and some horse books from Jessi. There was also a stack of hilarious snapshots Abby had taken at a recent meeting. Mary Anne had stuck in a poster of a kitten, and Kristy had added a key chain with a panda on it. Stacey sent a pair of very cool earrings, sixties-style daisies. The rest of the box was taken up with bags of candy — Hershey's Kisses, Peanut M&M's, and Twizzlers — plus wadded-up comics from the Sunday papers.

"Wow," Smita said. "You sure do have good friends."

"I know," I said, still feeling choked up.

Sarah put her arm around me. "You're lucky," she said. "Or maybe it's not just luck. Maybe you have a talent for making friends." She smiled at me.

That didn't help make the choked-up feeling go away.

"Have a cookie," I offered, holding the box out to them before I headed for the bathroom to blow my nose.

When I came back, Sarah and Smita were standing awkwardly by the door of my room. As soon as I walked in, I saw why. Alexis had returned.

"I guess we'd better head over to the library," Sarah said, giving me a look. "Remember? We were supposed to meet Jen there."

"Oh, right," I said, taking the cue. In fact, there was no such plan. But we were all uncomfortable around Alexis.

She barely registered my presence. A slight nod and a distant "Hey," were all she gave me.

I closed up the box of presents and left it on my bed. Hopefully, Alexis would leave it alone.

We hung out at the library until we were almost late for curfew. My room was dark when I returned, and Alexis had already gone to sleep. The box seemed to be just as I'd left it.

On Tuesday morning, I was up and out of the room early. Our math class was working on a special project that day: cooking corn muffins for the entire school's lunch. We were to meet in the kitchen right after breakfast.

The muffins turned out great.

The day did not.

Well, that's not entirely true. In fact, I enjoyed the rest of my classes on Tuesday. In French class Kerry read us a chapter from *The Little Prince*, in its original language. In global studies, my group had time to work on our project. Our short-story class was discussing a Flannery O'Connor piece. Creative Writing for the Stage was great, as always. Sarah and I were making lots of progress on our scene. Even gym was okay. The teacher, Mary Jo, was

125

starting us on yoga and I was learning to like it.

It was after classes were over that the day went sour. After spending an hour or so at the library, I headed back to my room to drop off some books and, hopefully, grab some time to catch up on my journal. I opened the door to the room and my heart sank.

This probably won't surprise you.

I don't know why it surprised me.

Alexis had demolished my care package.

The cookies were gone. The rest of the stuff was strewn all around the room. And the snapshots of my friends had been decorated with Magic Marker mustaches, devil horns, and black eyes.

I sat on my bed, clutching my stomach. This was it. She'd gone too far. I knew I should try to understand why she did the things she did, but I just didn't feel like it. I didn't care if she was angry, or unhappy, or jealous about the fact that I had good friends both at Riverbend and at home. I just didn't care.

I left things as they were and headed down the hall to find Pam. Fortunately, she was in. I took her to my room and showed her what Alexis had done. "I guess you were right," I told her. "We need to sit down and work this out. But she and I aren't talking much. Can you arrange it?"

That's all it took. Pam realized how serious the situation had become. By the end of the evening, she'd arranged a meeting for the next day, after classes. And Alexis had been informed.

Of course, she tried to apologize to me that night, but I refused to listen. "We'll talk tomorrow," I told her coldly as I turned out the light and went to sleep.

The next day seemed to drag by. For the first time at Riverbend I couldn't concentrate on my classes. Even Sarah and Smita couldn't cheer me up, though they tried their hardest.

Finally, after computer lab, it was time for our meeting. I walked into the conference room in the administration building to find Pam waiting — along with Jane Maxwell, the dean of students. I was surprised to see her there.

"I invited Jane because the situation seems to have become more serious than I thought," Pam explained. "When I saw your room yesterday, I — "

Alexis entered then.

"Welcome, Alexis," Jane said. She seemed pretty familiar with my roommate. "Let's all sit down, shall we?" She gestured to the comfy chairs that were ringed around a coffee table.

We sat.

Then we began to talk. Pam said that Alexis and I had not been getting along, then asked each of us to describe our relationship as roommates.

Ugh.

I didn't really want to be the one to start.

Alexis didn't seem hesitant at all. She jumped right in. "Mallory just doesn't seem to want to be friends," she said. "I tried, when we first met. But she buddied up with Sarah and Smita, and that was it for me." She looked convincingly sad. "I know there are things I've done that are not so nice. But I've apologized every time. Mallory just isn't very forgiving."

I nearly lost it.

"Not forgiving?" I asked. "How can I forgive some of the things you've done? And why should I? I was the one who wanted to be friends. But you've made that impossible." I knew my face was flushed, and I had to work hard to control my voice.

Jane stepped in. "Let's try to calm down a little, both of you," she said. "It's clear that something has gone seriously wrong here. I'm trying to understand what it is. Then maybe we can work toward a solution." She smoothed back her hair. "Now, let's start from the beginning. Alexis, how was it for you when you came back to school and met your new roommate?"

Jane guided us with gentle questions. Pam helped too. Little by little, the whole story came out. Only it was twisted, from my point of view. I explained that Alexis had claimed the room, read my journal without asking, borrowed my things, and tried to turn me against my new friends.

Alexis, in turn, did her best to make those things look like my fault. She truly seemed to see herself as the injured party, the one who deserved all the sympathy.

Would the dean and Pam believe Alexis — or me?

"There are a number of ways we try to solve problems like this," said Jane after our gripe session had ended. "Obviously, one solution is to rearrange the room assignments. But we try to avoid that, since it's the most complicated way to fix things. And we'd rather see interpersonal issues resolved than avoided." She paused, looking from me to Alexis. "So, here are a few other ideas. One, you can try to rearrange your room in order to minimize interaction. In other words, make each half of the room off-limits to the other roommate. Sometimes creating boundaries can help quite a bit in these situations."

Alexis rolled her eyes. "That's pretty immature, isn't it?" she asked. "We're not little kids."

"Okay, here's another idea," Jane volunteered. "You can draw up a schedule of 'room times,' so that each of you has time alone in the room that is guaranteed, every day."

That sounded good to me. I wouldn't have to tiptoe around, wondering if Alexis would be in the room or not. And I'd have time to write in my journal and read.

But Alexis was rolling her eyes again. "You know what?" she said, standing up. "I don't even want to hear any more of your dumb ideas. I don't care what we do. I'm out of here." She stormed out of the room.

I sat there, stunned. Now what?

Jane gave me a sympathetic smile. "I'm so sorry, Mallory. As you may know, this isn't the first time Alexis has been in this type of situation. We hoped that things would work out with you two, but perhaps we're past that point. I'll speak to the other administrators, and we'll see what we can do."

That made me feel better.

I headed back to my room, hopeful.

That feeling died the second I opened the door.

Alexis was trashing the place. Clothes and books were strewn all over the floor. Her bed had been moved to the farthest corner possible, while mine was in the middle of the room. The top of the bureau was swept clean, and its contents were flung far and wide.

"What are you doing?" I cried.

"I'm rearranging the room," said Alexis with a wild grin. "To minimize interaction." She threw a few more clothes out of the closet.

"I know it looks bad now, but once I'm done you won't even know I'm here."

"Alexis — " I began. I didn't know what to say.

She turned on me. The grin was gone. "That was a setup," she said angrily. "You and Pam are against me, and all you wanted was to turn Jane against me too. Now I'm in trouble with the dean."

"I didn't even know Jane was going to be there!" I protested.

Alexis wasn't listening. She continued to pull things out of the closet, then turned to the drawers.

What should I do? I had no idea.

Fortunately, Sarah came in at that moment. "What's going on in here?" she asked. "I can hear the commotion all the way down the hall." She took one look and took off. "I'll find Pam," she called over her shoulder.

Pam was able to calm Alexis down — or at least to convince her to stop throwing things around. But Alexis was still angry. She yelled for a few more minutes and then suddenly she stopped. I think she finally realized how bad things looked. There was no way Alexis could blame her behavior on somebody else this time.

She collapsed onto her bed. "I'm sorry," she said. "Oh, Mallory, I'm so sorry."

I didn't answer.

"I'll put your clothes away," she promised. "And your books. And everything. Just give me an hour, and I'll have the room back the way it was."

"No, thanks," I said. I didn't want the room the way it was. I just wanted to move out of there.

Right away.

CHAPTER 15

"Alexis, why don't you come with me," Pam suggested. "Let's go to my room and give Mallory some space. I'm going to have to call Dean Maxwell."

Alexis looked stricken, but she didn't argue. Meekly, she followed Pam out of the room, turning once just as she left to mouth the words "I'm sorry" in my direction.

I stood in the middle of my room, looking around at the wreckage.

"Whew!" Sarah exclaimed. "And I thought *I* was the dramatic one."

We laughed — though I felt dangerously close to tears.

Just then, there was a knock at the door. "Mallory? Is everything okay?"

It was Smita. And Jen. I opened the door and ushered them in. They stood and stared.

"Wow," Smita said.

"Oh, man," Jen added.

"I know," I said. "Hurricane Alexis just hit room nine."

A few other girls from Earhart showed up, and Sarah organized everybody into a cleanup crew. Within half an hour, the room looked pretty normal again. Everybody talked and laughed as they worked. The main topic of conversation was Alexis, and nobody had anything nice to say about her.

I was stationed near the bureau, folding clothes. I watched as everyone helped me out, repairing the damage Alexis had done, and I knew I was lucky to have found such good friends so soon after starting at a new school.

I thought about it. I'd only been at Riverbend for a week and a half, and it seemed as if I already had more friends than Alexis, who had been here for a *year* and a half. I never saw Alexis hanging out with other girls. She seemed to eat most of her meals by herself, study by herself, take walks by herself. Maybe she liked it that way — but I couldn't believe she did. Why did she have such a hard time interacting with people? I was still angry at Alexis, but just for a moment I honestly felt sorry for her again.

The room was almost back to its original state when there was another knock at the door and Jane Maxwell entered. She looked around at my group of helpers and smiled. "I see you have everything under control here," she said. "Nice job. Now, would you all mind giving Mallory and me a few minutes alone?"

"We're history!" Sarah proclaimed. She waved an arm and led everyone out of the room.

"Sit down, Mallory," Jane said. I sat cross-legged on my bed, and Jane sat on my desk chair.

"First of all, I think I owe you an apology," Jane continued.

I opened my mouth to protest, but she held up a hand.

"It wasn't fair to start you off at Riverbend with a roommate who was known to be — " she paused, "difficult." She looked down at her hands. "At the time we were making room assignments, it seemed easiest. And we knew from your application that you come from a big family and are used to sharing a room. We thought that if anyone could room with Alexis, it would be you." She sighed.

"I could try again — " I began.

"No, no," she said, shaking her head. "It's not fair to ask that of you. The situation has already gone too far."

"But how — " She'd already told me how complicated it would be to make a room switch.

"Under the circumstances, we're committed

to finding a way to accommodate you. Unfortunately, there's one problem. There are no empty rooms available right now."

Oh. So I was stuck with Alexis until a room opened up.

"However," Jane went on, "there is one possibility. I noticed that Jen Bodner was in here helping you clean up, so obviously you've already met her."

I nodded. "She's sort of a friend," I told Jane.

"Well, then you know she's currently living in a single room. If — and this is a big 'if' — if she were willing to give that room to Alexis and move in with you, our problem would be solved."

"I can't ask her to do that!" I protested.

"But I can," said Jane. "And I'm glad to. She can always say no. And if she does, I think you'll understand. It may just be that she prefers living alone. It's not necessarily a reflection on you."

I nodded. "Absolutely," I said. I tried to ignore the hopeful feeling that was rising inside me. After all, I knew that Jen liked me. But would she want to live with me? She'd have to give up a lot: space, privacy, a room all to herself. That would be crazy. Wouldn't it?

"I'll talk to her right now," Jane continued. "That is, if this idea works for you."

"Oh, it works just fine for me," I exclaimed. "Thank you!"

After Jane left, I lay back on my bed and closed my eyes. It had been a *very* long day, and suddenly I felt exhausted. I was too tired to do any more cleaning, too tired to write in my journal, too tired to pick up a book, too tired to think. I just lay there.

A knock came on the door. I sat up, my heart thudding. Was it Alexis? I didn't feel ready to face her.

Another knock. I stood up, walked unsteadily to the door, and opened it.

Jen was standing there.

Beaming.

"Hey, roomie," she said.

I started to beam too. "Really?" I said. "You don't mind?"

"Mind?" she asked. "Are you kidding? I was dying of loneliness up there. Sure, it was nice to have the space. But I'd much rather have a cool roomie."

That was me. I was the cool roomie.

Cool.

I couldn't have been happier. This was all I needed to make my life at Riverbend perfect.

A few nights later, I sat on my bed, journal in my lap. Jen was at her desk, working quietly. I looked around the room, enjoying the satisfaction it gave me to see my BSC collage on the wall, my things on my half of the dresser top. This room belonged to both of us, to me and Jen.

I began to daydream again, just as I had the night before I left Stoneybrook. Only this time, instead of picturing myself *leaving* a place, I pictured myself arriving.

I imagined myself flying high above the ground, soaring with outstretched arms as I took off from Stoneybrook and circled over all the old familiar sights before I rose and flew over Connecticut, over Massachusetts. I saw myself gliding toward Riverbend and steering straight for Earhart. Then I was slipping in through the window of room nine, where Smita, Sarah, Jen, Pam, and some other familiar girls stood waiting. (Alexis, I have to say, was not among them.) Jen was in front, holding a huge cake lit with bright candles. I pictured myself floating closer, in order to read what was written on the cake.

WELCOME, it said. WELCOME, MALLORY!

In my daydream, I read it out loud and laughed. The other girls laughed too, and told me to blow out the candles.

I did.

And I felt welcome.

Dear Reader,

For several months, Mallory had been having problems fitting in at school. She's a good student and she has friends in Stoneybrook, but she was unhappy and felt she didn't fit in at SMS. Worse, she felt her teachers didn't understand her.

The All-New Mallory Pike represents Mallory's successful struggle to find her place in school, even though it means changing schools altogether. Mallory's decision to leave Stoneybrook may have been surprising, but sometimes you just need a big change. I didn't go away to school until college, but when I did, I remember the exhilarating feeling of being able to start fresh. There's nothing like a chance to make all-new friends, meet all-new teachers, and try on an all-new life. It was a very exciting time.

Mallory's solution to her problems might not work for everyone, but it was the best choice for her.

Happy reading,

Ann M. Martin

L. GODWIN

Ann M. Martin

About the Author

ANN MATTHEWS MARTIN was born on August 12, 1955. She grew up in Princeton, NJ, with her parents and her younger sister, Jane.

Although Ann used to be a teacher and then an editor of children's books, she's now a full-time writer. She gets ideas for her books from many different places. Some are based on personal experiences. Others are based on childhood memories and feelings. Many are written about contemporary problems or events.

All of Ann's characters, even the members of the Baby-sitters Club, are made up. (So is Stoneybrook.) But many of her characters are based on real people. Sometimes Ann names her characters after people she knows, other times she chooses names she likes.

In addition to the Baby-sitters Club books, Ann Martin has written many other books for children. Her favorite is *Ten Kids, No Pets* because she loves big families and she loves animals. Her favorite Baby-sitters Club book is *Kristy's Big Day*. (By the way, Kristy is her favorite baby-sitter!)

Ann M. Martin now lives in New York with her cats, Gussie, Woody, and Willy. Her hobbies are reading, sewing, and needlework — especially making clothes for children.

Notebook Pages

This Baby-sitters Club book belongs to _____.

I am _____ years old and in the _____

grade.

The name of my school is _____.

I got this BSC book from _____.

I started reading it on _____ and

finished reading it on _____.

The place where I read most of this book is _____.

My favorite part was when _____.

If I could change anything in the story, it might be the part when

_____.

My favorite character in the Baby-sitters Club is _____.

The BSC member I am most like is _____

because _____.

If I could write a Baby-sitters Club book it would be about _____

_____.

#126 The All-New Mallory Pike

In *The All-New Mallory Pike*, Mallory makes one of the biggest changes ever in her life. I think Mallory's move away from Stoneybrook is _____ _____ because _____ _____. If I had to make Mallory's choice between Riverbend Hall and Stoneybrook, I would have chosen _____ because _____ _____. If I could go to school anywhere in the world, I would go to _____ _____. If I were going away to boarding school, the two people I would want to come with me are _____ _____ and _____ _____. If I could go to boarding school with any of the members of the BSC, I would go with _____ because _____ _____.

MALLORY'S

Age 2 —
Already
a fan of
reading.

Age 10 —
Still a fan.
Waiting to
meet my
favorite
author.

SCRAPBOOK

Two of my favorite things— babysitting and Ben.

My family— all ten of us!

Read all the books
about **Mallory**
in the Baby-sitters Club series
by Ann M. Martin

Look for #127

ABBY'S UN-VALENTINE

"So, you *do* agree that romance is not a bad thing," Ross said.

"We'd made it to the hall. Time to go to math class. Since I didn't have a perfect homework paper to flaunt in front of Ms. Frost, I didn't mind lingering a little. "Romance is not a bad thing, in its place."

"Like the Valentine's Day Dance," Ross said.

"Yeah, I guess," I conceded.

"So you want to go?"

"Go where?" For a moment, I thought Ross was talking about class. Then I saw him duck his head.

"To the dance," he said to his feet. "With me."

"The Valentine's Day Dance? Here at SMS?" I was incredulous.

"Yes," he said.

"No," I said.

He looked surprised. He looked taken aback. He looked hurt.

Maybe I'd been a little rude. "Ross," I began, "I truly don't buy into all this stuff. Nothing personal, but I'm just not that kind of person."

"Yeah, I know," he said, recovering. "Just checking."

"Did I pass the anti-romance test?" I joked.

"Yup."

"Good. I have to go. See you," I said.

Feeling a little weird about our exchange, I turned and walked toward math class. I happened to look back just before I turned the corner.

Ross still stood there, staring after me.

In my mind, I began composing a new sonnet. It was called, "To Valentine's Day" and it began, "How do I detest thee? Let me count the ways."

100 (and more) Reasons to Stay Friends Forever!

More titles... ➧

The Baby-sitters Club titles continued...

☐ MG22877-3	#93	Mary Anne and the Memory Garden	$3.99
☐ MG22878-1	#94	Stacey McGill, Super Sitter	$3.99
☐ MG22879-X	#95	Kristy + Bart = ?	$3.99
☐ MG22880-3	#96	Abby's Lucky Thirteen	$3.99
☐ MG22881-1	#97	Claudia and the World's Cutest Baby	$3.99
☐ MG22882-X	#98	Dawn and Too Many Sitters	$3.99
☐ MG69205-4	#99	Stacey's Broken Heart	$3.99
☐ MG69206-2	#100	Kristy's Worst Idea	$3.99
☐ MG69207-0	#101	Claudia Kishi, Middle School Dropout	$3.99
☐ MG69208-9	#102	Mary Anne and the Little Princess	$3.99
☐ MG69209-7	#103	Happy Holidays, Jessi	$3.99
☐ MG69210-0	#104	Abby's Twin	$3.99
☐ MG69211-9	#105	Stacey the Math Whiz	$3.99
☐ MG69212-7	#106	Claudia, Queen of the Seventh Grade	$3.99
☐ MG69213-5	#107	Mind Your Own Business, Kristy!	$3.99
☐ MG69214-3	#108	Don't Give Up, Mallory	$3.99
☐ MG69215-1	#109	Mary Anne To the Rescue	$3.99
☐ MG05988-2	#110	Abby the Bad Sport	$3.99
☐ MG05989-0	#111	Stacey's Secret Friend	$3.99
☐ MG05990-4	#112	Kristy and the Sister War	$3.99
☐ MG05911-2	#113	Claudia Makes Up Her Mind	$3.99
☐ MG05911-2	#114	The Secret Life of Mary Anne Spier	$3.99
☐ MG05993-9	#115	Jessi's Big Break	$3.99
☐ MG05994-7	#116	Abby and the Worst Kid Ever	$3.99
☐ MG05995-5	#117	Claudia and the Terrible Truth	$3.99
☐ MG05996-3	#118	Kristy Thomas, Dog Trainer	$3.99
☐ MG05997-1	#119	Stacey's Ex-Boyfriend	$3.99
☐ MG05998-X	#120	Mary Anne and the Playground Fight	$3.99
☐ MG45575-3		Logan's Story Special Edition Readers' Request	$3.25
☐ MG47118-X		Logan Bruno, Boy Baby-sitter	
		Special Edition Readers' Request	$3.50
☐ MG47756-0		Shannon's Story Special Edition	$3.50
☐ MG47686-6		The Baby-sitters Club Guide to Baby-sitting	$3.25
☐ MG47314-X		The Baby-sitters Club Trivia and Puzzle Fun Book	$2.50
☐ MG48400-1		BSC Portrait Collection: Claudia's Book	$3.50
☐ MG22864-1		BSC Portrait Collection: Dawn's Book	$3.50
☐ MG69181-3		BSC Portrait Collection: Kristy's Book	$3.99
☐ MG22865-X		BSC Portrait Collection: Mary Anne's Book	$3.99
☐ MG48399-4		BSC Portrait Collection: Stacey's Book	$3.50
☐ MG92713-2		The Complete Guide to The Baby-sitters Club	$4.95
☐ MG47151-1		The Baby-sitters Club Chain Letter	$14.95
☐ MG48295-5		The Baby-sitters Club Secret Santa	$14.95
☐ MG45074-3		The Baby-sitters Club Notebook	$2.50
☐ MG44783-1		The Baby-sitters Club Postcard Book	$4.95

Available wherever you buy books...or use this order form.

Scholastic Inc., P.O. Box 7502, 2931 E. McCarty Street, Jefferson City, MO 65102

Please send me the books I have checked above. I am enclosing $_____
(please add $2.00 to cover shipping and handling). Send check or money order—
no cash or C.O.D.s please.

Name_____ Birthdate_____

Address _____

City_____ State/Zip _____

BSC1297

THE BABY-SITTERS CLUB®

by Ann M. Martin

Collect and read these exciting BSC Super Specials, Mysteries, and Super Mysteries along with your favorite Baby-sitters Club books!

BSC Super Specials

BSC Mysteries

More titles ➡

The Baby-sitters Club books continued...

❑ BAI47050-7	#12 Dawn and the Surfer Ghost	$3.50
❑ BAI47051-5	#13 Mary Anne and the Library Mystery	$3.50
❑ BAI47052-3	#14 Stacey and the Mystery at the Mall	$3.50
❑ BAI47053-1	#15 Kristy and the Vampires	$3.50
❑ BAI47054-X	#16 Claudia and the Clue in the Photograph	$3.99
❑ BAI48232-7	#17 Dawn and the Halloween Mystery	$3.50
❑ BAI48233-5	#18 Stacey and the Mystery at the Empty House	$3.50
❑ BAI48234-3	#19 Kristy and the Missing Fortune	$3.50
❑ BAI48309-9	#20 Mary Anne and the Zoo Mystery	$3.50
❑ BAI48310-2	#21 Claudia and the Recipe for Danger	$3.50
❑ BAI22866-8	#22 Stacey and the Haunted Masquerade	$3.50
❑ BAI22867-6	#23 Abby and the Secret Society	$3.99
❑ BAI22868-4	#24 Mary Anne and the Silent Witness	$3.99
❑ BAI22869-2	#25 Kristy and the Middle School Vandal	$3.99
❑ BAI22870-6	#26 Dawn Schafer, Undercover Baby-sitter	$3.99
❑ BAI69175-9	#27 Claudia and the Lighthouse Ghost Mystery	$3.99
❑ BAI69176-7	#28 Abby and the Mystery Baby	$3.99
❑ BAI69177-5	#29 Stacey and the Fashion Victim	$3.99
❑ BAI69178-3	#30 Kristy and the Mystery Train	$3.99
❑ BAI69179-1	#31 Mary Anne and the Music Box Secret	$3.99
❑ BAI05972-6	#32 Claudia and the Mystery in the Painting	$3.99
❑ BAI05973-4	#33 Stacey and the Stolen Hearts	$3.99
❑ BAI05974-2	#34 Mary Anne and the Haunted Bookstore	$3.99
❑ BAI05975-0	#35 Abby and the Notorious Neighbor	$3.99
❑ BAI05976-9	#36 Kristy and the Cat Burglar	$3.99

BSC Super Mysteries

❑ BAI48311-0	Super Mystery #1: The Baby-sitters' Haunted House	$3.99
❑ BAI22871-4	Super Mystery #2: Baby-sitters Beware	$3.99
❑ BAI69180-5	Super Mystery #3: Baby-sitters' Fright Night	$4.50
❑ BAI05977-7	Super Mystery #4: Baby-sitters' Christmas Chiller	$4.50

Available wherever you buy books...or use this order form.

Scholastic Inc., P.O. Box 7502, 2931 East McCarty Street, Jefferson City, MO 65102-7502

Please send me the books I have checked above. I am enclosing $ _____
(please add $2.00 to cover shipping and handling). Send check or money order
— no cash or C.O.D.s please.

Name_____Birthdate_____

Address _____

City_____State/Zip_____

Please allow four to six weeks for delivery. Offer good in the U.S. only. Sorry, mail orders are not available to residents of Canada. Prices subject to change.

BSCM1297